# The Autumn Effect

Rachel Ann Chrostowski

Art Director: Parker William Lenz
Cover Design: Bryan Miguel

G. Lenz Publishing
Printed in the United States of America

First Printing

ISBN: 0-6922-1075-X
ISBN-13: 978-0-6922-1075-8

# DEDICATION

This book is dedicated to my best friend. The path to completing this
novel will be a story I will never forget.

# CONTENTS

# ACKNOWLEDGMENTS

Maybe in a way far too similar to Dan's, the memory of where I first found the spark that developed into the story within these pages is still unclear. There is no doubt who told me a truthful story that was intriguing enough to remain on my mind for days and weeks. However, when I asked about it later, this person had no recollection of the events. Maybe this story is *my* Jamie.

# I

Opening scene. A boy sits at a library desk that could seat six. Books lay sprawled all around him; a notebook lies out in front of him and a coffee to the side. He stares at the notebook, his fingers bouncing a pencil up and down against the fine white paper. His eyes are unwavering, in fact they haven't moved in five minutes. The pencil keeps on bouncing; the pages do not turn and the air grows hotter, as if the anxiety of the all the students in the library was filling up the building with unbearably hot air. The boy keeps staring at the title he has at the top of his notes: *Psychology 230*. The only thing was that psychology wasn't on his mind, in fact, far from it. In attempts to form any sense of creativity, he had begun to narrate his life as if it were a movie. It had become a failed attempt.

*What the hell am I even doing here?* The boy thought. The only response was a girl sniffling two tables in front of him. With his head bowed he glanced over the bouncing pencil towards the girl. She sat completely immersed in a novel. Her feet balanced on the chair next to her, and her backpack, phone, and music device strategically placed in a simple arc on the table. She sat with the novel in one hand, her other hand bearing a pen to her lips, which she had unconsciously chewed on. The boy had a sarcastic grin on his face as he watched the girl. *Perhaps she'll take a huge bite out of that pen, and the ink will explode all over her face.* The boy chuckled at his thought, which immediately reverberated all along the library walls, the chuckle carrying itself to the girl who was reading. She glanced up over the yellowed pages, took the pen from her lips and then went back to the novel.

The boy became bored with the girl who couldn't realize that her cute method of reading was in fact annoying as hell, and looked back down at his notebook. Nothing had appeared in the time that he had looked away. His eyes trailed over to the huge textbook that he had drawn from his backpack. The cover had swirls of colors and large lettering, as if the cover alone had the sole purpose of sucking a student into reading the whole damn thing willingly. The human brain wasn't a thing to be read, but rather explored and discovered. *Guess there isn't a better way for us to do that than through boring lectures…awesome.* Against the glare of the lights that hung above his head he noticed a greasy fingerprint plastered to the hard cover. The boy took his hand, wiping it against his jeans, and then dutifully wiped away the fingerprint. Proceeding to open it, he flipped to the middle of the chapter that his professor was currently lecturing in. He stared at the words and paragraphs, the graphs and the pictures. His professor's voice suddenly droned in his head and the letters in the text became numbers and the numbers strange encrypted symbols. *I can't even concentrate on a single paragraph!* The boy slammed the book shut. Again, the sound made the reading girl's head snap up, and another girl who was perusing through shelves to look over at him. The girl standing in between the shelves gave a slight smile, as opposed to the reading girl who glared with her tiny eyes over her book.

The pencil began bouncing against the paper again, and this time the boy moved his attention to the coffee cup. It was the simple pasty white cardboard, the kind of cardboard that if he scrapped his fingernail along the side it carried the effect of nails on a chalkboard. The brown sludge within it though was his main concern. Even the caffeine that was supposedly contained in there didn't withhold any magical effect on him. In fact, even within those few minutes of picking and poking at the inanimate objects in front of him, he realized that the half a cup of coffee that he already consumed hadn't give him a jolt of renewed energy what so ever. He had begun to draw doodles on the cardboard when another student entered the study room. The new student held himself in such great regard that narcissism could be personified, pooling off of him like a wave of water. He picked the table in between the boy and the reading girl, slamming his bag against the wooden desk. He looked around, chewing loudly on his gum before sitting down. A sudden buzz emanated from his pants, and he hurriedly pulled out his cell phone. Flipping it open, he pushed the phone against his ear.

"Hey what's up? Naw, I'm in the library," he said without a whisper. The boy who sat doodling on his coffee cup had a disgusted look on his face, to which the girl still browsing shelves smiled slightly at. *Why the hell would you come here if you're just going to talk on your phone?* The boy's judgmental thoughts floated all around him as he set the cup down, realizing that the coffee had since become ice cold and wouldn't even be able to satisfy his empty stomach or fulfill its purpose of rejuvenating his crushed mind.

The boy turned to his notebook again. At the top where it clearly read *Psychology 230* the boy took his pen, crossing the words out till they were a big black blur. He then replaced it with the title *The End of My Life as I Know It.* The boy dropped the pen next to the abandoned pencil. He bent over, placing his tired head in his hands. He rubbed his eyes vigorously, sitting back up in his chair but leaning down and placing his head on the table. His eyes followed the large swirls of the notebook rings and soon drooped lower and lower until he felt his mind completely shut off.

A cry echoed in his ears. A thunderclap struck the entire sky and lightning blinded the whole world. He stood on the edge, drifting ever closer to it with tender footsteps. The wind was quick, a fierce rush that pushed him inches closer. He peered over the edge and saw nothing but a dark, cavernous hole. The howl of the wind laughed at him as he tried to step further and further back, but his feet only drew closer and closer to the edge.

*Pebbles dripped from off the rock wall, sinking into darkness. The cry entered his ears again, a sharp piercing that reverberating along the rock wall, causing more pieces to dismantle themselves into the depths below. The wind still pushed and pulled him at full force. His arms were held out at his sides, the only part of his body that held balance.*

*The cry rang out again, just as lightning struck feet away from him. Sparks and drops of fire sprinkled themselves over his legs. The clothes burned away but the fire did not singe his skin. The cry was released again, and he curiously looked down at the canyon depths again. The cry was coming from below, thousands of feet away from him, but it was the strongest and loudest sound amongst all the chaos around him. It could have been the cry of an infant, or the shout of a man, he couldn't tell. The sparks of lightning continued to rain down on him, but yet he felt no pain. The storm around him grew. The clouds became thick, the wind an epic torrent of power that took over everything around him. The fire still trickled all along his torso, but he couldn't feel a thing. All he knew was that the cry kept calling for him, begging for him. It couldn't be quelled.*

*His eyes were now locked on the darkness, his arms still opened wide to fight the battle that was all around him. He kept staring into the darkness, and heard the cry that filled his entire mind. His fingertips played with the snatches of wind that wound itself through his outstretched hands. The fire still licked away at his clothes, but his skin remained unscathed. He looked up at the thunderous, turbulent sky. He felt nothing.*

*And then he jumped. His body flew silently through the wind, which carried him closer and closer to the darkness. The cry came closer and closer to him as darkness soon engulfed his body. The fire was no longer there; the lightning and thunder had disappeared. All that was there was the dark canyon, the cry and his body, floating into the abyss. Death gripped him at full measure, and all he could do was to smile.*

His head snapped up. The library's light was suddenly too bright. The noises of pages turning, footsteps stomping and pencil's erasing was an endless drone in his mind. It took a moment for him to realize that he had stopped breathing and with a swift gulp he took a fresh breath of air and exhaled it quickly. His mind still reeled from the dream. He looked around but no one seemed to notice that he had been asleep, or that he had just as obnoxiously woken up with a start. Still breathing heavily, he rubbed his hands along his face, a small pool of sweat had gathered against his brow. He stuck his knuckles into his eyes, watching the red and green lights appear on the inside of his eyelids. Calming his body down, he looked back down at his notebook. It was just as blank and forgotten about as before.

*Screw this,* he thought, tossing the books and notebook quickly into his bag. He stood up gingerly, his body slacking in exhaustion. He grabbed the cup of coffee, glancing up to see the boy who had been talking on his cell phone now browsing the internet, and the girl still completely lost in her novel. Sauntering out of the study room, his coffee was haphazardly thrown into the garbage, a hushed crash as the coffee seeped out of the cardboard cup that bounced off the bottom of the bin. The boy continued walking out of the library, thinking about the dream, the work that still sat in his bag, and the fact that he hadn't properly slept in three full days. For a brief moment as he exited into the cool, dark night, he wondered if it would be worthwhile to narrate his life again.

"So tell me about what you believe in?"

"What the hell kind of question is that?"

"Do you believe in God?"

(Pause)

"I guess I do…"

"Do you?"

"Well yeah, I mean if God has everything set out for us in his big plan, then I guess I have to believe in him in order to get through all the bad stuff that happens…all for the greater good I guess you can say."

"So you believe in determinism?"

"What?"

"Determinism, the idea that everything we do is predestined, non-negotiable."

"Sure."

"It's just a thought. So why do you think everything is set out for us?"

"Cause I hate making choices."

"Is that the real reason?"

"No, it's the only snide thing I could come up with at the moment." (Pause) "I don't know, I guess I believe that because then it's easier to know that nothing can be helped, nothing can be changed. I mean, look at a car crash. It's easier to accept that people died in a car crash knowing that there is nothing that could have been done about it."

"What if the people had been able to avoid the crash in time?"

"Then that's what would have happened. Simple as that"

"Alright then, let's take a more mundane approach. You picked psychology as your major-"

"Glad to know that's a mundane topic."

"I'm sorry; I didn't mean it like that."

"It's okay; it's just good to know that what I plan to do with the rest of my life is mundane. Makes my life look *really* good."

"Again, I didn't mean it like that. I only meant to drift away from such serious topics like human beings dying in a car crash."

"Why? Human beings die every single second of every single day. We still carry on our lives without difference, so why does it matter if we talk about it so nonchalantly?"

"I think we're diverging onto something else entirely."

"That's true, we originally were talking God, and then somehow threw philosophy into it, and now we're talking about the dullness of human life. So which original topic are we going back to?"

"What I was going to ask is that did you have a choice to pick your major?"

"Course I did."

"Then it wasn't set out in the bigger plan. You chose to major in psychology. So how does that work with the 'bigger plan' of determinism?"

"How the hell should I know? It just does. For my mind, it seems like I willingly picked psychology. If it was determined that I should have picked a different major than I would have."

"That simple?"

"Yep."

"So you don't have freewill?"

"What do you mean? Not if everything is determined, then no."

"So for instance, we'll go back to the interesting topics, what if someone wanted to kill him or herself. Is that determined?"

"Yes."

"So what if something hinders them from succeeding?"

"That was bound to happen."

(Pause)

"Well...."

"Scary thought isn't it? That we can't control anything. But in reality, we can't."

"So tell me Dan, how does that help you live? Knowing that everything is destined and fated to happen, that it cannot change."

(Pause)

"It doesn't help. In fact, it makes life totally worthless, bullshit."

(Pause)

"That's why half the time, I don't feel anything."

"What do you mean?"

"I mean that I feel nothing, believe in nothing."

"Well, that's not a life to live then."

"Damn right it isn't."

# II

He is walking down a street that he knows will end. Eventually he will face the wall in front of him, turn around, and walk back from the same way that he came. The question now becomes why does one walk down that street in the first place? Why walk down a dark alley if it exudes only more darkness and fear? Does the street provide an answer? Instead of being endless, can one finally face the truth instead of continuing to walk and walk with no conclusion? Or rather, it is seen as being a path that makes people turn back, unable to face what lies ahead of them? Is the street that he knows will end a dead end, or an ability to turn back and take one more chance?

The thoughts that whirled through Dan's mind contained everything from the sleep that he yearned for; to questioning whether or not what he was doing right now had any purpose at all. He knew it was the exhaustion taking over his mind, but every single time he walked past a building, he found himself staring for a few minutes at the empty black space that existed between the two immense structures. A part of him wanted to walk down the dark path; another mocked him for thinking that the darkness withheld more meaning than what it was in actuality: just a dark pathway that would be lit up by the sun the next day. Still, he hung on every minute or so, staring into space, the music blaring inside his ear drums from the player that hung in his coat pocket. His fingers wrapped themselves around the strap of his bag; his other hand constantly switching the song to one that would suit his mood, but nothing in particular replaced his own thoughts that were spinning in his head.

He lumbered back to his apartment, taking the steps slowly as he jingled the keys out of his pocket. Above were the sounds of music and shouting as parties and gatherings erupted from the windows. Smoke trickled over from the group of people who stood feet away from the apartment doors, the muffled whispers being dulled even more so by the blaring of the stereo systems above. A window that stood open above Dan allowed for guitar strums to exit into the air, along with the stench of weed. Dan sighed, turned the key and entered the building. He took the stairs carefully, feeling the weight of the entire day and of his hefty bag of books taking him closer to the ground.

*I'm one of the only people on this campus not getting completely trashed tonight,* Dan thought miserably. *How pathetic is that?* He came closer to the old wooden door that read 415 in stained gold metal numbers, and immediately heard the sounds of clanking cups, laughter, and music emanating from his apartment. Holding in his instant disdain, he opened the door with a swift turn of his key. A blur of faces greeted him as he entered, each person holding some type of alcoholic beverage in their hands and each with the growing stupor that the drink provided stamped on their faces. One of his roommates, a tall lanky boy who wore clothes that were ten times too big for him, sat on the couch with two other people playing video games. His other roommate had a girl strapped to his side as they muttered nonsensical words in the kitchen, one hand constantly refilling the girl's drink, the other perfectly placed around her waist to prevent her from falling over. Dan stomached the scene with a sense of grave serenity, and continued to walk on down the tiny hallway to his bedroom.

"Hey Dan!" his roommate from the couch shouted, barely even glancing up to see if Dan was even listening.

"You're finally back! Grab a beer and come join us!" The invitation was barely heard over the music, the crashing of cars that came from the video game, and the girl who stood next to Dan. He realized very quickly that she had one of the loudest and most obnoxious laughs in the world. He took every precaution to not even make eye contact with her as he ignored the living room's festivities and sauntered on.

A group of girls had meandered into the small hallway, a standing line that was waiting for the restroom. The girls all glanced over at Dan as he began to push through them, trying desperately to reach the last door at the end of the hall. A couple of the girls were giggling with nothing to say, another couple of girls whispered behind the cups that were hiding their lips as they looked him up and down. All Dan could think of though was how foggy his mind had become and how much sleep he wanted to get. Finally coming upon his door, he swung it open and proceeded to shut it loudly, and instantly turn the lock. He slammed his bag down right then and there and took the last few steps that yielded to him his bed. His body slumped down face first into the bed, his hand gripping the soft pillow and wedging it underneath his head. His mind seemed to completely shut off and all he could muster from his body was an effort to roll over and pull the blanket over him. His eyes turned to the ceiling and with a sigh of frustration, his eyes suddenly were open wide. All the sleep that he had yearned for wouldn't come for hours, despite what his tired body screamed at him. Dan felt his fingers clench around his blanket, his jaw clasp shut. Shakes coursed through his body as he bit back frustration. *What the hell is wrong with me?* He threw off the blanket, sitting up numbly. For a second he held his hands out in front of him. His hands were dry, with uneven fingernails that were chewed to the end and cut up skin around them. The sight was one of the most unhygienic things he had seen in a long time, but he realized then that he was beyond caring. It didn't matter how much he tried to will his body to fall asleep, or will his mind to stop the screwed up dreams he was having and just rest. It was already a hell of a school year, and it had barely begun.

The hallway was less packed as he reopened his door. Two girls were chatting, the drinks dipping downwards from their hands. One had her head leaning against the wall, her legs constantly readjusting as she tried to secure herself against the wall. The girl across from her glanced up at Dan. A smear of makeup underneath her eye could have ruined the entire ensemble that she had spent hours putting together. But as Dan walked past her he realized that he only highlighted her eyes even more, which were still aware and had a dagger like quality to them as they pinned Dan down.

The living room still was a mass chaos of bodies roaming in no direction at all, but rather shuffling from one place to another ever so slightly. The music erupted once more over the numerous conversations that were occurring, creating an instant stab of pain in Dan's head. His roommate who had been sitting on the couch was now lumbering over to the fridge. Dan, paying little attention to anything around him but realizing that his mind was still forcing him to do something while his body screamed in fatigue, came up behind his roommate.

"Jesus Dan! Way to sneak up on me!" his roommate quickly jumped out of the way as Dan mumbled an apology, reaching into the fridge and grabbing his own drink. "You okay man; you look really out of it."

*Out of it? What does that even mean? Is my mind somehow disconnected to my body? Cause that's definitely not happening right now. In fact, pretty sure the two are having an all-out battle with each other for the rest of the night.* Dan looked up to his roommate, feigning a smile as he cracked open the beer.

"Just glad it's the weekend man," he quipped. The sarcasm was missed on the roommate, who just grinned and began chugging the drink in his hand. Dan rolled his eyes, moving his way back to the living room towards the couch that held a vacant seat in the middle. He plopped down into the couch, the fabric sinking even further from age and use. On one side sat a girl who held a cup in between her legs as she furiously texted on her phone. On the other side was a girl, who sat talking to a guy that was leaning over her with his hands on the arm of the couch. Her smile and laughter were forced, and Dan chuckled softly as the guy kept trying and trying to make any sort of impression. He took a sip, and knew that the mood of the night would drastically change.

The rest of the time he spent on the couch was a blur. He was a frozen image, whereas everything else around him was moving at a cranked up speed. The girl texting soon left with her friends in an angry huff. The guy trying to impress the girl ultimately failed as the girl soon got up with an excuse that she had to use the restroom and then never returned. A couple had sat down next to him, expressing their emotions to the entire room as they began fervently kissing. Another girl sat down and began talking to him, and it wasn't until minutes into the conversation did he even realize someone in the room was interacting with him. The girl promptly left with an angry glare. Dan felt himself stand every few moments to grab another drink, and soon the cans were littered on the coffee table in front of him. But still, the feeling that as he stood still and the room around him spun in fast motion stuck with him.

He soon realized with pure enjoyment that the psychosis and human condition the exhibit of a group of college students were not only completely deplorable, but also simply ridiculous. The couple next to him soon paused in their exchanging of saliva and eventually, unaware of Dan next to them, began fighting. Another girl managed to make it to the couch, only to pass out and then have her friends pick her up and drag her home. Dan watched every single movement and action made by everyone in the room with a sarcastic grin on his face, and a cynical look in his eye. Every single action made tonight was an account of drinking, many of them probably would never have occurred in a sober social situation. His roommate who had been clinging to two girls eventually retreated into his bedroom with one of them. Dan could only imagine the various situations that could come from that and all it made him do was laugh. The scene was hilarious and disgusting. Everyone around him, including himself in his own stupor, had drunk his or her thoughts and inhibitions away. And tomorrow it would all come crashing back in blasting headaches, upset stomachs, and realized mistakes. It was an endless, deadly, stupid cycle, and all Dan did was laugh at it.

There was one moment that Dan couldn't forget amongst all the pandemonium around him. A moment came when he looked up, and he saw a girl in the corner. She had curled blond hair that hung past her shoulders and her face was slightly shadowed by the walls around her. Dan sat there dumbfounded, for there was nothing truly distinct about her features, and there was nothing more that he could see since she had hid herself in the dark. But one thought still ran through his head: *I know her. How do I know her?* It was a moment of pure déjà vu, for no matter how hard he wracked his brain, he couldn't think of a moment in which he would have seen this girl before and remembered it so vividly. In a second of a person walking between them, the girl had turned her back to Dan and exited the apartment. A part of Dan wanted to stand up and run after her, see whom she was. But the other half of him was already planted into the couch, numb from all the drinks he had. She had looked at him before she left, and he had let her go. It was such a crystallizing moment, one that Dan wouldn't be able to get out of his mind for days. He looked down at his beer, which had been hanging limply from his hand. He finished the last sip, and felt the warm liquid leave a disgusting taste in the back of his throat. His body stood up, and he stumbled back to his room. The music had died, the people had slowly disappeared back into the streets, and a harsh silence had fallen over the entire apartment. Dan felt his eyelids droop more and more as he lay in bed, and now he almost wished he could stay up a little bit longer. He wanted to figure out where that girl had come from. But soon sleep took over, and he dropped the cup he was still holding onto. The cup bounced on the floor, and landed on its side. The last drops of the drink ran down the white inside of the cup, and soaked into the gray carpet.

"Why did you pick psychology as your major?"

"I want to know how the mind works."

"You want to know how the mind works. So, do you want to continue on as a psychologist?"

"Don't know yet."

"Well, what about psychology are you interested in then?"

"I feel like I'm answering your questions more than once."

"What about the mind do you want to study?"

"Why people do what we do?"

"Elaborate more on that."

(Sigh)

"Okay. I want to study why people enjoying eating, why some people like running, and some people like playing videogames instead."

"Well, some of these questions already can be answered."

"Fine, then let's go for the ones that can't. Why do people enjoy hurting other people? How does the mind wrap around torturing other human beings? What about killing someone? Why do people do that? How about fucking someone? Huh?!?"

"There's no need to get angry Dan."

"I'm not getting angry; I'm just tired of wadding through all the small talk. That's really what I want to study, the destructive and bizarre human nature of the mind."

"Well, the people who exhibit those actions and thoughts are not psychologically healthy Dan."

"Why not?"

"If these people are hurting others, then they are harming

society--"

"So that's it then, isn't it? These people are deemed unfit by society."

"For good reason Dan, they're unhealthy destructive behavior hurts others."

"But why does society get to deem them unhealthy?"

"I beg your pardon?"

"Why does society get to make the call? In fact, it's really not even society who made that call. It's a bunch of people who think that they're better than everyone else so they get to dictate what's right and what's wrong. If society had a factor in it at all, we'd still have weekly gladiator fights to the death to weed out the population."

"But those battles were sometimes used to have criminals fight each other, the people that were deemed unfit by society."

"So what you're saying is that the government has always had control over what people can do?"

"No, what I'm saying is just playing devil's advocate against the theory that these people could be fit to interact with other people."

(Pause)

"So what about a college kid who drinks himself to death? Is that technically a destructive behavior? If he makes it out alive is he then deemed unfit for society?"

"It's not the same as someone killing someone else."

"Yes it is; he was killing himself with alcohol. What about a woman who eats so much that the doctors say she will die of a heart attack, yet she keeps eating. Isn't she being destructive?"

"She still can be helped. And it definitely doesn't carry the same weight as someone murdering others. That carries more with that person than an eating disorder. Dan, your argument has digressed away from the original question of why you're studying psychology."

"I know. We seem to be doing that a lot, don't we?"

"Well, we certainly should get off the subject of the government and society."

"Why? I'm still interested in that topic."

"Dan—"

"What about a girl who refuses to eat because she wants to stay thin, *based* on the images of women give to her by social culture? Is she deemed unfit?"

"Dan, I will stand by my statement that there are many differences between psychological problems that can be fixed, and psychological problems that leave a person mad and damaging. This has nothing to do with society anymore. Yes, society does dictate a lot as you say, but what can also be said is that the term 'deemed unfit' is used to describe the people whose minds are not normal, whose minds have been altered and changed, making their psychology and psychosis different than others. It can often be treated, but it can often be harmful, and that is why they are placed where they cannot hurt others. A man who imagines things that aren't real has a disorder that makes reality a distant idea to him. If a man can't even connect in reality, how are they to function in this world?"

(Pause)

"Are you telling me you've never imagined anything that wasn't there?"

"Have you Dan?"

(Pause)

"Would that deem me "unfit for society"?

"That's not what I'm asking Dan."

"No, but that's what I'm asking."

# III

Pencils scribbled along the notebooks while typed keys resounded against the walls. Each person in the room hung onto Professor Arnsteen's every word as he tried to make the subject at hand as entertaining as possible. Everyone in the room would look up to see his expression and then frantically look back down to try and remember what he had just said. The man spoke with a quality of voice that was hard to ignore, a calm resonating voice that flowed throughout the room, accompanied by the faint scent of arrogance.

Dan was a few sentences behind now, and would remain that way for the remainder of the lecture. His mind was still completely dead from the weekend, his body still aching from lack of sleep and proper food. The cell phone next to his notebook lit up with a faint greenish hue, and the white letters announced that Dan's mom was on the line. Dan glanced at the phone, looked back at the board, and continued to tap his pen lazily against the notebook. Face buried in his hand, he leaned further and further down towards the desk, his eyes drooping more and more. His phone lit up again, signaling a voicemail, which would once again include the worried voice of his mother.

It would be the third call in two days, since Dan had refused to come home and eventually had begun the inevitable decline in calling his parents at all. The original phone call was the night after the party, in which Dan had been passed out on his bed for hours, the persistent ringing finally entering his clouded brain. The buzzing phone eventually caused Dan to rise from his state of throbbing and fatigue, fumbling as he hit the *call* button and awkwardly placed it to his ear.

"Hello?" it was practically inaudible and hoarse. The other line paused for a moment before his mother finally mumbled a word.

"Dan? It's three o'clock in the afternoon! Are you just waking up?" Dan winced at the worry that clearly dripped from his mother's mouth. He rolled onto his back, his stomach turning instantly.

"It was a long night Mom." The light breaking through the blinds sent knives through Dan's mind. Fingers braced against his forehead, he took a deep breath and willed the churning in his stomach to stop. "What's up Mom?"

"Well, you haven't been home in two months and—well your Dad and I were hoping you could come for a visit. It's your Father's birthday next weekend you know."

The ability that his Mom had to go from worrisome parent to a nagging nuisance still astounded Dan. *And she wonders why I was so excited to move out?* Dan's head lolled as he moved the phone away from his head, taking a deep sigh.

"Dan, are you even listening to me?"

The phone was back against his ear the next second. "Yeah Mom, I'm listening. I don't know if I can come home this—"

"Do you really have something going on this weekend? Are you really going to tell me you can't come home for your Dad's birthday Dan?"

Dan swallowed back every angry thought that suddenly had bloomed in his mind. He felt his jaw clench, shifting back and forth till his forehead was splitting from the doubled pain of his anger and from the hangover that raged his entire body.

"Dan…are you okay? Is everything okay at school?"

Dan couldn't give those questions any more thought than he already had. *Of course I'm not okay; everything is fucked up in life right now, even though in reality there's nothing in my life at all! And school is crap. Always has been. Always will be.*

"Yeah Mom, I'm fine. Just a long night.

"Well, tell me you'll think about this weekend." It was his

mother's way of a guilt trip, and truth be damned Dan knew he probably wouldn't be able to say no.

"Of course, Mom. I got to go though. I'll talk to you later." The phone snapped before his mother could say another word. The next moment Dan was dragging himself to the bathroom, the place he spent the rest of the day in.

Arnsteen's voice shot through the blank slate that was Dan's mind, bringing a moment of his attention back to the lecture that he had now completely ignored. Notebooks were slammed shut, pens chucked into bags. Phones snapped open and jingled back to life, and headphones already blared with music as people filed out of the classroom quickly. Dan clumsily took his head from his hand, shaking off sleep as he glanced down at his notebook. There was nothing there, no trace of his mind being at this place at all. Rather just the empty body that he had managed to lumber over from his apartment. Dan watched as people stood up, either frantically running to another class, or acting just as passive as Dan, who couldn't care less whether or not he even finished the other classes of his day. He carelessly threw his notebook in his bag, pocketing his phone without a second glance at the voicemail that continually flashed again and again as a constant reminder, and stood up, looking at the last person who was leaving the room.

Her blond hair wasn't curled, but rather haphazardly put together into a messy ponytail. He caught the profile of her face, in which he noticed that her eyes were always roaming, aware of everything around her. For a brief moment, her blue eyes met his, and Dan realized that he was probably gawking at her. The moment of déjà vu had set back in, and he couldn't help but try to stare at her in order to finally figure out who she was.

Her eyes quickly looked him up and down, and Dan was startled to see that they held a slight sadness in them that seemed to have lasted for years. As suddenly as Dan realized that he was staring at her, she just as rapidly turned away and was out the door. Dan stood, completely dumbfounded, his backpack slipping from his shoulder.

"Bad day?" Arnsteen was leaning against the table, his arms crossed with a slight smile stamped on his face. Dan immediately was shaken from his reverie, and gathered up the rest of his things. Arnsteen was a character, a man who knew that girls in his classes loved his smile, and that taking the boys from his graduate classes out for a drink always made for a great night. Dan couldn't pass on Arnsteen's classes; the man was an utter genius in Dan's eyes. Many office hours were filled with discussions not only about lecture but also any random topic that Dan could think of, for Arnsteen had a way of knowing everything that Dan wanted to talk about and was always filled with the energy that was addicting to watch and participate in.

"Eh, it's nothing. You know how weekends are." Arnsteen's laugh filled the entire room.

"That's very true. Though I must say I missed having you in class today." Arnsteen arched a brow. It made Dan feel more disappointed than when his own Mom tried a guilt trip on him.

"I'm sorry Professor. I'll catch up right away—" Dan's face instantly turned red, and he fumbled with his backpack and shirt sleeve all at once. Again, Arnsteen flashed an award-winning smile, placing Dan into ease.

"I know you will, don't give those bullshit excuses. Besides, Wednesday's class will be exceptionally interesting, at least I think so. You better get ready," Arnsteen said as he began gathering up the papers that he had sprawled all over the table over the course of the lecture. Dan felt himself lingering by the edge of the doorway, and he knew that he had only one once chance to ask what he wanted to.

"Professor?" Arnsteen stopped, looking up at Dan sincerely. "Who was that girl with the blond hair that left before me?" Arnsteen's puzzled look made Dan instantly regret the question. "I just…I saw her the other day and was just curious."

"Her name is Jamie," Arnsteen curtly answered. Dan nodded licking his lips fervently and trying to rid himself of the embarrassment that crept all over him. He mumbled his thanks and reached for the door. "Dan?" Dan's body swung back around, almost afraid to look Arnsteen in the eye. "Don't do something stupid."

The coffee that Dan had instantaneously drunk after class not only created a jittery sensation in his fingertips, but also an acrid taste in his mouth. Dan sat slumped in the bench of the coffee shop, watching people file in and out, practicing boring small talk with one another, and rushing for another class as they snatched their drink from the counter. The bustling college campus outside yielded only more students and faculty. People talked on their cell phones, chatted with others on the streets, even pushed and plowed through others in order to cross the street.

Dan couldn't help but imagine everyone around him like a cloud of ants running around confused and deranged, following a tight knit schedule in which the slightest thing going wrong meant that the entire day was ruined. The drone of the music from his headphones was the only thing keeping him alert to what was around him, while his leg had begun shaking from the huge amount of caffeine he had consumed in such a short time. Everyone around him seemed to have a purpose. Dan however, was content sitting at the spot that he had been for an hour, listening to music and turning what could have been friendly glances at people into awkward stares as he watched everyone who came in. He wasn't doing anything at all, he was completely without purpose. And it was the most relaxing afternoon he had for weeks.

"Dan!" A friend suddenly broke the satisfied state that Dan was in, walking directly up to him and giving him a friendly shake. "How's it going man?" Dan nonchalantly nodded.

"It's going, I guess."

"Yeah, I hear you. Did you still want to get together and go over things before the test on Friday?" Dan wasn't about to admit that he had completely forgotten about the test. He wasn't worried about the test. He easily could look over the pages of notes once or twice and be fine. His friend across from him however, was expertly signaling that he needed all the help he could get.

"Yeah man, of course. I'll give you a call."

"Sounds good, I gotta run to class. I'll talk to you later." And just as quickly as he arrived, the friend was gone, his jacket licking the edge of the doorway as he briskly walked away. Dan watched for a quick second, when suddenly another figure caught his eye. It was the girl from his psychology class who had walked through the doorway. She hardly gave Dan a second glance as she walked to the counter. Her fingers slipped into her bag and then pulled out a wad of cash, which she dutifully unfolded and neatly placed on the counter as she paid for her coffee. Dan watched over the edge of his cup, chewing on it fervently while trying not to have anyone notice that he was staring directly at this one girl.

Her footsteps were light and particular, as if she were calculating every step that she could. Dan took a hesitant lurch forward, then paused. *What the hell would I even say to her?* It was daunting, but it was also daring. Dan found himself suddenly standing up, following Jamie out of the store. The clean glass door could have shattered from the heavy sound of the street life. Buses and cars honked, birds called overhead, and people shouted to others across the street as they ran into different stores, or across the street towards academic halls.

Dan for a brief moment lost her, frantically turning a full circle before catching her at the end of the block. The streetlights changed from yellow to red and Jamie came to complete halt at the edge of the sidewalk, taking a quick sip of coffee. Dan inched closer and closer, wildly looking around to keep his mind occupied. *What is wrong with me?*

A bus came close to the corner, causing Jamie to once again take another step back. Dan paused, twenty feet from her. Her blond hair was picked away from the ponytail from the sudden burst of wind that flowed through the street. A stray pile of leaves wound around Dan's feet, catching against the sides of jeans and then snapping back into a dance as they fluttered away. He stopped, and the world around him followed with. Jamie turned, a lock of hair catching around her neck. Dan reeled back, and felt his breath catch. He blinked, but the scene didn't change. Fear gripped his entire body, a clammy, cold sensation washing over him.

Jamie's face held only one color, and it was a dark crimson that covered her whole entire face. Her eyes were still visible, but glazed over. No life was sustained in them, but rather had been completely drained. Dan finally sucked in a breath, his whole entire chest practically collapsing in on itself. Dan knew that the blood that covered her face was no illusion, no matter how much he willed it to. It wasn't a trick of the light; it wasn't his mind finally giving in to the exhaustion that clung to his body. It was real, and he would fight to the end to convince himself otherwise. *What the hell is going on?*

Jamie brushed her hair away from her face, fixing her eyes onto Dan. Her face was once again clean and fair. Her eyes still held liveliness, but also the same self- reproach that Dan noticed before. There was a story within the guilt that Dan saw, but the rest of her belied what her eyes were tragically trying to express. Again, he became frozen, astonishment planted on his face. Jamie's eyes quizzically looked at him, and then turned away. The world lurched back forth again. People suddenly passed Dan at fast speed, the bus drove quickly past Jamie and she took a step forward as she crossed the street. He felt his feet drag him across the street. He hardly paid attention to what was surrounding him, but rather focused on her. She turned a sudden corner and he followed. And just as suddenly she disappeared. Dan stopped in shock within a few paces around the corner. *What is wrong with you Dan?*

"Why are you following me?" Her voice forced him to turn around. She peeked from the corner of an ugly brown alley that held two garbage bins. Steam escaped from the vents above, the pungent smell of food escaping into the air. She stepped back, her arms crossed in protection. Her face was hard, her eyes square on Dan, seething with warning.

"I—" Dan wished he knew what he could say, but no words came out. The caution melted from her face as she sensed the discomfort that Dan had placed himself in.

"If you wanted my notes from class you could have just asked. It's not like you were paying attention today anyways," her slight smile was calm and relaxed.

"I'm so sorry, I know this looks weird," Dan had found his voice again, and now realized that he wasn't going to stop until he completely explained himself. "I think I saw you at a party at my place the other night and I just…Have you ever had moments of déjà vu?" A small chuckle and all the fear in Dan escaped him.

"It's a real bitch let me tell you that," Jamie replied. "But yeah, I have."

"It's just, I had that feeling the other day and again in class. I didn't mean to chase you down the street, I was hoping to catch you after class and…" his voice still was wildly nervous. He had no idea what he was doing, or why he was doing it. He just knew that he needed to see her, speak with her.

"It's okay." She still hung back, and he sensed the lack of trust that she still had towards him.

"I'm Dan, by the way."

She chuckled again, hiding her face briefly behind her hair before tucking it back behind her ear. "Is this always how you introduce yourself to people?" Dan still stood dumbfounded, now sickened by what he had actually just done.

"Jamie."

They paused in silence for a moment, her face silently judging him, while his face still tried to contain the embarrassing agony that was now this scene.

"Well," she started, cautiously slinking away from back from the direction that she had come from. "I guess I'll see you in class on Wednesday?"

"Yeah." Dan couldn't utter another word, but only watched her go. The déjà vu was gone, and that feeling would never return whenever he saw her again. But the image of her standing in front of the bus would stay with him the rest of the day. He had stared death right in the face, and she had seemed totally submissive with it.

"We haven't talked in quite some time."

"I've been busy."

"How's school going?"

"It's the same thing every day. Lecture after lecture, followed by homework, followed by a few miniscule hours of sleep. Rinse and repeat."

"You don't like school?"

"I don't like the monotony of it."

"Do you do anything extracurricular?"

"Does drinking really count on a future resume…No I don't do any other activities."

"Why not? Wouldn't it help to get a job? Make some extra money. Outside activities can help with meeting new people."

"I thought that was the high school speech that they gave everyone."

"The same can apply for college students. It's a different set- up, a harder transition."

"I'm halfway through my junior year. I have friends."

"It was just a suggestion Dan."

(Pause)

"I know. It's just not me to walk into a new room and introduce myself to strangers. If you randomly talk to people they think you're crazy, but yet that's what everyone expects you to do. It's a Catch-22."

"It is. But sometimes that what helps create friendships, jumping outside of your comfort zone and talking with people you normally wouldn't."

"I met a girl from one of my classes."

(Shifting sound of movement on the couch)

"Do you have a girlfriend Dan?"

"No."

"When was the last time you dated someone?"

"I had a girlfriend in high school; we broke up a few weeks after my freshman year. I've met other girls, but I don't want a serious relationship or anything."

"Why not?"

"It's not something I want on my mind."

"Do you see a serious relationship as hard work?"

"Don't you?"

"Nothing worth keeping is easy."

"Well fine, then I haven't found a girl I really like, okay?"

"There's no need to get defensive Dan."

"I'm just sick of all these personal questions! Why does it matter if I have a girlfriend or not?"

"It was just a question Dan."

"Yeah, well it's not I'm this anti-social person who can't talk to people. You try talking to people these days! Everything is so god damn fake most of the time. It's a farce and everyone in this world falls for it. People think that they have one good night together at a party and that they're best friends when they leave. I doubt names are even remembered the next day. And it's not like I haven't met girls! I mean there is Jamie—"

"Who's Jamie?"

"A girl from my Psychology class."

"The one with Arnsteen?"

"Yeah."

(Pause)

"And how is she?"

"She's cool. We've talked in and out of class."

"Dan. Nothing said here leaves the room. You know that?"

"Still doesn't mean I'm sharing every detail of my life with you."

"I'm not asking you to do that Dan. It's just easier to know what's going on in your life so that we can figure out—"

"Figure out what's wrong with me? Because supposedly I'm a fucking psycho!"

"Your mother is worried about you Dan."

"That's because moms always worry. It's not just her either; it's the rest of the world. It's you. It's every professor I've had, my parents, and my younger sister. Everyone worries. I have a duty to complete, a list of things that people expect me to accomplish by the time I graduate. Well guess what? That list that everyone has for me to check off probably isn't going to happen! Deal with it!"

"What list Dan?"

"It's a series of expectations. I have to have a girlfriend because then I should be getting married. I have to have a steady job. I have to think about grad schools. I have to do everything and it's all deemed by everyone else around me. Nothing is a decision on my part."

"You know that many people you're age feel this kind of pressure."

"Really? Then how come I feel like I'm the only one suffering?"

(Pause)

"Exhibit A. College boy confused, just like everyone else."

(Pause)

"I'm done talking with you today."

# IV

It's a funny thing to walk around a campus during a week of midterms. Any visiting student would think the campus was quiet, the people boring, and the huge weight of a straight week of testing humiliating and torturous. The sudden transformation from a Saturday night to a Sunday morning before tests is a sight to behold. The nonsensical noises of Saturday night are quenched by the students' hushed anticipation of the tests that will arrive Monday. The rush of blasting music is silenced by the calm surrender inside the library's walls. But there's also the frantic and feeble scramble to learn everything that was missed out in the first weeks of school. Memories of parties, late nights, and nonchalant evenings suddenly are replaced by futile attempts to memorize every lecture that had been instead filled with much needed naps and texts about future lunch dates.

And much to the dismay of his roommates, who were dreading every minute that dragged them closer to midterm week, Dan felt a calm tranquility fill him instead. Most of his professors had canceled the extra day of class, and two in particular were skipping class early for the upcoming break, kindly making the previous test the midterm grade. Therefore, Dan was left with literally three hours of tests, no extra lectures and an amazing outlook on the tiny but much needed break ahead of him.

Whereas so many people stressed over the week, Dan sat amused with a textbook haphazardly opened to a random page at his side. His roommates and friends all locked themselves in quiet, claustrophobic corners, but Dan instead lounged on the couch, rereading his notes every so often. The convoluted college lectures already contained countless information that Dan didn't need to know, plus he also was fortunate to have the professors that dictated exactly what was on the midterm, making studying almost hopelessly impractical. And though it was only an extended weekend of a break, Dan still looked forward to the four days when he could do absolutely nothing.

The end credits to a movie scrolled up the screen, and Dan who was sunk deep into the twenty year old couch that resided in his apartment, was picturing the boardwalk that led to the beach near his house. The tall grass would still be there, along with the chilling breeze as fall rolled in, and the distant sound of waves, even though the ocean was only hundreds of feet away. It was one spot where Dan could escape from everything, his family and school included; even the residents of the area, who ignored the secluded spot for their own portion of the beach that was their backyard.

As Dan sank further into the couch, trying desperately to reread the page of notes that he had been staring at for over thirty minutes, this was the place he thought of. It was only four days out of reach, and yet it seemed like a lifetime would have to pass before he made it back there. The constant lull of classes had begun to take a toll on Dan. Besides the brief moments that he had managed the courage to talk to Jamie, an interesting conclusion came to mind. Even as he sat here, determined to set in some hours of studying, he realized that nothing else really mattered to him right now. The conversations with Jamie left something to be desired, and no matter how much he tried to overlook the feeling, he still would glance at Jamie every so often, trying desperately to remember from where he knew her. Nothing yet had come to mind.

*Okay Dan, you can do this. Only a few tests, nothing major.* Dan picked up the notebook, the pages curled from use, the notes already fading from being paged through too many times. *Just look over your notes a few more times, and you'll be fine.* But the words became constant blurs, messages that suddenly couldn't be encrypted anymore by human eyes. His body was heavy, his eyes hurting. In fact, Dan realized that his head was suddenly throbbing beyond belief. With a mind that wasn't able to comprehend anything for the rest of the night, his eyes drifted towards his cell that lay along the cushion next to him. Before he knew it, his phone was flipped open, and his fingers were furiously texting.

Dan: *Hey Jamie, what are you up to?*

He dropped the phone back down, immediately picking the remote back up, aimlessly flipping through channels of absolutely nothing. Dan's goal was to not worry about the text, the thought directed behind the text, the fact that deep down he wanted nothing more than to hang out with Jamie for the rest of the night, but he felt himself glance back and forth from the television to his phone every minute. It was with a huge breath of relief and a swift grasp of his phone that it lit up after only five minutes.

Jamie: *Studying in the library, huge test tomorrow. Care to join?*

The invitation was there, it was blatant and it was worthwhile. No strings attached, no hidden messages within the words. It was simple and direct. And for that very reason, Dan felt himself numbly set the phone down, ignoring the message from Jamie. His head was splitting and in all honesty he wanted nothing more than to fall asleep until his class tomorrow, regardless of whether or not he was even ready for the test. Jamie could be excited, eagerly waiting to see him show up at her desk. She also could be callous and indifferent, just another boy trying to buy more time with her.

He wanted to take a chance, but was too afraid. Instead, he was willing to let himself not take the chance, suffocating himself with possibilities that all ended in heartlessness to his own self. His head felt like it was going to crack in two, and even though his phone lit with another message from Jamie, Dan felt himself instead manage to haul up the rest of his body onto the couch, watching the blurry images of the television fade into his mind.

*The air was thick. Enormous, stormy clouds yielded nights of perpetual rain, and the endless growth of every plant in the area. Tonight seemed extra hot and stuffy. In reality it was only sixty degrees with the threat of a thunderstorm lingering in the air. Dan slowly trudged back to his apartment. He didn't even know how late it was. What he did know was that if he carried this backpack any more he was going to collapse in the middle of the sidewalk due to exhaustion. And if he didn't get rid of the headache that raked every portion his body he was going to yank his eyeballs from his head in order to stop the pain. It was always the same shit, every single day. And he was tired of it all.*

*A group of girls passed him, breaking away from their gossip since Dan didn't even notice that he was going to barrel right through them. All he could think about was making it up the stairs and falling straight into his bed. He turned the corner to the next street, two blocks away from his apartment. The laughing from the girls faded away till it was just the sound of distant traffic that remained. He could see the apartment, but suddenly it seemed that with every step he took, it dragged him two steps back. The trek to his apartment seemed forever away, stretching further and further from him. He paused, taking in a deep breath, glancing up at the sky. Gray clouds swirled above him, with the faint light of the moon pushing through the clouds. It was a surreal moment. Everything around him was still and unreal, frozen in a momentary pause. There was no sound, no human life, there was nothing.*

*But in a split second, Dan had a sense of foreboding. When so many would feel the cold stream of consciousness sweep over them, Dan instead felt sweat pool over his entire body. A wave of exhaustion crept through his body, his knees buckling under him.*

*A stifled shout suddenly issued forth from an alley feet way from Dan. His body snapped up in alertness. There were the common sounds of scuffling being released from the darkness. A woman's scream was muffled, and her body was slammed against the red brick wall. Dan felt his fingers trace along the cold wall, inching close towards the dark alley. His fingers bent along the cracks in the wall, tracing along the drips of grime and mold that clung to the brick. He edged close, and the shouts of the men made him freeze.*

*"Shut up and stand still!" Her cries were shielded, but images of the men taking advantage of her were all Dan could think of. The cold wall quelled his sweating body. He had nothing to hold onto, nothing to clutch. All he heard*

were the men's laughs and leers, and the girl's panicked cries. His eyes blurred with tears, his lungs unable to grasp any air. His eyes peered around the corner of the wall, and his body slumped down as low to the grimy ground as it could.

The girl was pinned against the wall, the two men wearing dark jackets, tattered jeans. One had stringy hair dripping with sweat, clinging to his unshaven face. The other had a worn baseball cap over his cropped hair, a sneer gathering along his whole face. Dan watched the girl's eyes flit back and forth, frantically looking for a way out. One man had both of her arms clamped to her side, the skin of her wrists bitten by the hard brick and issuing out drops of blood. Her face was panicked, her eyes wide with fear.

The other man stepped closer, reaching into his jacket pocket. A glint withdrew from the black leather. The man grinned, a chuckle escaping his lips. The girl's eyes fell on Dan.

The sound that was made was something that no ear should ever hear. It was the sound of metal scrapping against the hardest substance a body could carry, easily breaching the layer of soft tissue that protected precious organs. Her clothes were ripped and her skin seemed to seamlessly open towards the knife. For a brief moment the knife was lodged, stuck. It was only with another forceful thrust that it sunk even deeper. A bone broke; one could hear it cracking from beneath her skin. And just as forcefully, the knife was withdrawn. Her eyes were still fixed on Dan, this time the muffled hand unable to suppress the screams that rang forth. Her eyes held every single emotion, every thought and feeling. Nothing could have prepared her for this, and nothing in this world would every repair or mend her. The knife was crimson, glinting in the streetlight.

The next second was the most fascinating image that one could ever witness. For that tiny, miniscule moment, her body seemed perfectly fine. There was no wound; there was puncture against her perfect ivory skin. But just as quickly as the moment passed, suddenly blood pooled from the lesion. A gaping hole suddenly gushed blood as it ran down her stomach, dying her jeans and seeping onto her legs. The knife began its work again. The screams soon died, as the chokes of breath could be heard from under the man's hand. The bones still cracked, the skin still ripped. The wall was dyed red, exceeding its already crimson color for a newer, more prominent hue.

Dan had watched the whole thing. His lungs began to tighten. His eyes *could not, would not waver from the girl. His knuckles were white as they gripped the edge of the brick wall, the corner beveling away at his skin as he raked his palms back and forth. His body was a tight ball of seized muscles, unable to move. The color of her eyes seemed to fade, and just as slowly did her body finally slump down to the ground. The man dropped the knife from his gloved hand, bending down over her. It was finished, and all Dan did was watch.*

*A sudden urge to move backwards caused the sharp scrap of a stone against the concrete sidewalk. The two men swiftly spun around, seeing the lonely young man creeping around the corner.*

*"Hey! What the hell?"*

*Dan's body suddenly wasn't frozen. The cold senseless awakening of his body brought him reeling back towards reality. His body was up, and his feet were sprinted back from the direction that he came in.*

*"We'll get you, you bastard!"*

*Her body still lay there, slumped and unresponsive. Her bright eyes were fading in luster. Her hands were curled at her side, her fingers almost beckoning for someone to come and find her. Her head was cocked to the side, masked over by the dark shadow of night. The brightest color on her was now the blood that gathered all over and around her, making her picturesque, and strikingly beautiful. It was the image that remained in his mind's eye.*

Dan woke with a start from the dream, a startling scream escaping his lips. He paused, his stomach rolled and he ran for the bathroom, retching from the miserable experience and the image that his mind tortured him with.

"You're not saying much today Dan."

"There's nothing much on my mind."

"There must be something that you would want to talk about. What about this girl you mentioned last time? Jamie. How is she?"

"She's fine."

"Just fine."

"Well what do you want me to say, I don't know where she is every minute of every single day! We're not dating anyways."

"Just a question. Does it upset you that you're not dating?"

"Wouldn't it upset you if there was a girl that you liked who could easily look right past you without a second thought?"

"Well, why don't you take an initiative in dating her?"

"Tell that to every other person trying to date in the world today. I'm nothing to her. I'm just another guy that she talks to in between class. I mean nothing to her, which is how so many other people in this world view me."

"That's not entirely true Dan. There are many people who would see you as a meaningful part of their lives. Your parents, family, close friends. Even Jamie, though you have only known her briefly, would probably say that you mean something."

(Pause)

"If I walked into the sea, would anyone take notice? Would anyone even stop me?"

"Why are you asking that Dan?"

"Just answer the question."

"Of course someone would notice. If someone saw you they would stop you."

"Would they though? What if I was alone, no one else around me?"

"Why would you be at the sea alone?"

"Because that's the most relaxing scene ever. Wouldn't you want to be alone at the sea, without the screaming children and shouting parents around you?"

"But if it's relaxing, why would you try to kill yourself?"

"Who said anything about killing myself?"

(Pause)

"That's what you assumed, isn't it?"

"Yes, it was actually. I'm sorry, Dan."

"It's okay. The reason it's relaxing is because I've never seen death as scary. Even in its darkest moments, it always ends in some form of peace. Walking into the sea, yes, eventually my body would be immersed in water, and yes, eventually my lungs would twist and convulse for air. But the feel of water surrounding you, like a blanket, and the sight that you see before you actually step into the ocean, there's the peace that remains with you to the end."

"You have a very interesting perspective on death."

"Is that a compliment?"

"It's just what I want it to mean Dan."

"Oh."

(Pause)

"Have you ever noticed that if people are right in the face of death, or watching someone dying, and they do absolutely nothing?"

"Dan, I don't think this is something that we should talk about."

"Why not? It's on my mind."

"Fair enough Dan. Why do you think people just watch death?"

"Because they're amazed. Because they could help but they're too transfixed by what they're seeing. Everyone can image death, or someone dying. But once it actually faces you, suddenly you're aware of nothing else."

"Interesting view, once again. Do you think of this a lot Dan?"

"Recently I guess."

"Why?"

"Have you ever had a dream that seemed so real you could sworn it was?"

"Of course. So it was a very lucid dream?"

"Yes."

"Is that what sparked the conversation for death and dying?"

(Pause)

"Did you see someone die in your dream, Dan? Or did you die?"

(Pause)

"Dan, even in your dreams, I would appreciate to know

about things like this. Suicide is—"

"It wasn't suicide okay. It was someone getting killed." (Pause) "Murdered."

"Who was it? Do you know?"

"No. I kind of wish I did, maybe. No one should have to see that. I know it was a dream, but still…it…it seemed so real."

"Perhaps it means—"

"Please don't try to analyze this dream. It is what it is."

"Would you like to talk about it more?"

"Not really. I vividly saw a girl get stabbed against a brick wall. It seemed so real that I puked everywhere when I woke up and felt like shit for the next three days. Why would I want to talk about it more?"

"It was just a thought Dan—"

"If someone were to ask me why the brick was so red, I'd be able to answer. It's because of the girl who was killed there. Do you think I'm joking? That I'm using the color red as a metaphor for blood? You have no idea how red blood really is till you see it drip from an innocent person's fingertips. Red is blood – and that's all it'll ever be. Take a look at that brick wall again. If you see the bloodstains, well done. Now you know why brick walls in this world are red. It's from all the senseless murders that occur in a fucked up world!"

"Dan! Calm down! This dream wasn't real!"

(Pause)

"Real or not, that doesn't stop the image from haunting my mind."

# V

An impenetrable pounding was stuck in his chest, unceasing and unyielding. It shook his whole body, clinging to every bone with immeasurable weight. He was a cracked, fragile shell that was on the brink of shattering at any second. Shards would fly in all directions, the deep, pounding core inside of him being all that remained.

It was an image. An image on an endless reel. This image was what caused his body to tremble. The lights around this image would dim; the audience would wait in anticipation. The audio would begin to play; the visual would begin to move, frame by frame. A dark alley appears only lit by the faint glow of moonlight and artificial street lights. The audience becomes curious, leaning forward in delight at what the screen could show next. The camera turns ever so slowly, a continuous shot that grips the viewers. The camera slows, and light fades onto the crumpled mass. A red stain saturates the brick. The audience laughs at the body, her face plastered in fear. The red is a ghastly shade, too crimson for the audience to take seriously, so the laughter continues.

Dan knows the truth though. The reality is that the blood is very red because it's fresh. It was an image, but it was one that wouldn't fade now that it had returned. He couldn't remember how long he had sat in that bathroom. It could have been hours or just mere minutes, it didn't matter to him. All he knew was that his stomach couldn't stop rolling, and his throat couldn't be relieved of the tangy taste that was left from throwing up. Dan couldn't even remember the last thing he ate, let alone drink in order to be so sick.

In essence, he knew it was all from the dream he had, though for the life of him the images had all disappeared. He glanced at his shaking hands that clung to the edge of the sink. Nothing prompted the dream to return. It all was just a hazy cloud that hung grimly over his head.

A splash of water along his face and Dan walked out the door. The clock hanging against the living room wall caught his eye, telling him that only ten minutes remained till class. *Shit!* Dan frantically grabbed his bag, stuffing notebooks and his phone into it before running towards the door. His roommate leaned against the counter, lazily sipping from the gallon of milk that he held in his hand.

"Hey man, just about to wake you for your class," Dan mumbled inaudible words, his stomach leaping in distress. "You were out really late last night." The last remark stopped Dan, making him reel around.

"What are you talking about? I was crashed for hours," he said incredulously.

"No man, you came in at like five in the morning, really loud too. Must be why you look like hell today."

Dan didn't know what he hated more, his asshole of a roommate or the fact that the last time he remembered was one in the morning.

The sun was out but the day felt cold. All Dan could think in his head was a quote that described the world being a museum of immense strangeness. *Who the hell said that?* Dan realized his mind was a blank slate, containing no well-rounded conscious thought. *Fuck, what the heck happened last night?* He forcefully dragged his body towards his class, where Arnsteen was certain to see the massive torment that was consuming Dan. The campus had an eerie feel to it. Dan briskly walked past those who looked just as sleep deprived as he, those who looked just as freaked out as he did and those who were silent in relief, having just finished the last of their exams.

Dan carefully dodged one person to the next, trying to catch the shortest route to his classroom. The academic buildings seemed to glitter in the sun, majestically leaning over the students with years of knowledge and experience. The rest of the world looked gray, the sun being sucked up by the campus. Even peoples' faces seemed gray, reflecting not the sun but the dread that was on Dan's face. The dream wasn't as hazy anymore. Noises could be heard, scuffling and struggling sounds. There were three people, two men and a girl.

Dan reached for the door. Her face suddenly slammed into his memory. Her eyes were glass; they contained every answer but withheld no reprieve. Liberation was in the distance, and she had no way of reaching it.

"Well, nice of you to show up Dan." The door calmly clicked shut as Arnsteen's voice broke into the fog that was in his head. The face was gone.

Dan was done with the exam. It lay limply along his desk. He had finished it with incredible ease, the only test he placed any value on and the only one he found worth studying for. The clock ticked away fifteen more minutes, and more and more students filed out around him. He wanted to be the last one, and from the occasional glance from Arnsteen, his professor knew that too. His eyes now were centered on the window, looking beyond the glass to the people that were scattered around outside.

A group of men stood directly in front of his view. One held a coffee, another a briefcase and the third held one of the most arrogant smirks Dan had ever seen. They all were talking slowly, no smiles or laughs. It was the heavy, grayish air that stopped them from enjoying the conversation. Dan sat with his pen twirling in his fingers, staring at the men. The one who sipped coffee suddenly turned his head, catching Dan's gawking face. All three pairs of eyes were on him. Dan felt a disturbing shiver run down his back. He quickly looked ahead towards the blank chalkboard. They say that a person calms down by concentrating on something else, but no matter how much Dan turned his pen in his hands, his eyes still wanted to wander back to the man. He took a hesitant breath, his eyes focusing back towards the window. A pair of eyes still lingered, burning into Dan's back.

He quickly rose from the desk, watching out of the corner of his eye with frantic paranoia, the last student briskly placed the test at the end of Arnsteen's desk. Dan himself mimicked the other student, quietly laying the test down, his eyes centered on the scratched paper where he had written his name. *Dan Braddock*. He stared at it for some time, as if his name held a superior significance than just the justification that this was indeed his test. But it didn't. In fact, as he stared at his name more and more, the name sounded duller and plain.

"Dan?" His head snapped up. Arnsteen's hand covered up his black printed name. Dan looked at his professor straight in the eye, and immediately looked back down, anywhere but at his professor, whose eyes already were roaming for an answer. Dan still felt eyes on him, a pair beyond those of his professor's. They were constantly watching, unwavering in their stare.

"Everything all right? You look…scattered." Dan focused back on his professor. Arnsteen's face showed genuine concern, and held a hesitance that left the conversation completely impressionable. Dan felt himself stop, breath, open his mouth and then shut it again. He glanced away, back towards the window, where the burning feeling originated from that bore into his back. The men were gone.

"Professor, have you ever had a dream that felt so real, you could have sworn it was true? Or…what about one that you wish you could remember, but couldn't?" Arnsteen began packing up tests and papers, slipping them into his bag with such ease that Dan began to feel a coolness swarm him.

"Very good questions Dan; dreams are always a fun lecture."

"I'm not talking about lecture topics for when we get back, I understand the psychology of dreams! I want to know if…if you've ever had a moment when a dream felt real…"

Dan felt his voice rise and fall with his growing frustration as images and snippets came crashing back into his mind. "…That maybe it actually was?" The silence in the room was palpable, strained by both the men in the room who avoided each other's gaze. Arnsteen took a deep breath, his lips pursed and his jaws clenched.

"Dan? Did something happen?" Dan looked back at the window. The man with the coffee was back, talking fervently on his cell phone. He could have been talking about the happiest occurrence in the world, but regardless his eyes were plastered in raw aggravation. And suddenly, they looked back towards the window, directly at Dan. A wave of anxiety washed over him. It was the cold, red brick that covered his entire vision, being cleansed spotless by the wave that still bore down on him.

"Dan?" The feeling was gone, the wave had crashed, and the silence still remained in the air. He took a breath. The air was cold, that was all that Dan could muster in thought. "Dan?"

"I'm sorry. I just…I just had a late night." Dan felt a laugh escape his lips, one that he was forced to muster. Arnsteen gave a slight smile, wishing to be confident and sure of Dan's expression, but he knew that something was hidden. Something was deeply harbored. "Have a nice break."

His bags were packed, his phone lay next to him, and everything in the apartment was absolutely still except for the quiet hum of the television. Dan's eyes were glazed over in exhaustion, his head buried halfway against the cushion of the couch. His body ached, his mind was closed to everything around him, but the flutter of images still rattled no matter how much he tried to put it out of his mind. He watched the pixels of the television change, darken and brighten again. The laughter that emanated from the character within the screen didn't attract Dan; it didn't stir him from his position.

His phone suddenly sparked to life, buzzing against the fabric of the worn couch. Dan picked it up, his eyes barely able to focus on the name on the screen.

"Hello? Yeah…yeah I'm ready to go. No, I'm just tired.

Yeah, I'll be down in a minute." He slipped his phone into his pocket, grunting as he stood up. He quickly snatched up his packed bags and laundry, flipping his keys in his hand as he looked around for any forgotten item. The door clicked shut and he was jumping down the stairs two at a time. It was space that he needed. It was space from the campus, from the constant commotion, or the constant monotony, whichever way one would want to look at it. His mom was waiting at the edge of the sidewalk, a cheerful smile on her face. His mother held an exuberance that always had a way of altering the moods around her. Her laugh was contagious; her smile was wide and always bright. She gazed at Dan with excitement, elated to have her son back even for just a few days. Giving one of the biggest hugs she could muster, she enveloped Dan in her arms.

For that brief moment, Dan felt all the anxiety around him melt away. He didn't need to worry about anything anymore, about the tests, the schoolwork, or the dream. It was only a dream, and by the growing night, a new dream would fill Dan's head. The mother and son climbed into the car, the soft chortles of music streaming from the stereo. The car jerked forward and Dan's mom began to drive away from the gray apartment, away from the hushed campus. Dan watched the street lamps passing in perfect consistency. An empty street suddenly appeared, littered with various items of trash that moved slowly with the wind that swirled all along the outside walls of the building. One red brick wall stuck out in Dan's mind, and his eyes were frozen on it till the car drove far enough away that the wall disappeared from view. The brick was perfectly stained in a new shade, like a new coat of paint on the wall.

"You're very quiet today."

"I have a lot on my mind."

"Well, now's the time to share it."

(Pause)

"What was your first experience with death?"

"Dan, this is a very serious topic."

"I know. I still want you to answer the question."

"It was my grandpa. He had a heart attack."

"How old were you?"

"I was ten. Dan, I feel that we should move on to a different topic--"

"Did you notice that your view of the world changed after someone close to you dies?"

"What do you mean by that?"

"There's this memory...I'll never forget it either. I was eleven. My family lives near the coast, you see, but there's also a woods near our area. My older brother and I would always bike out there. One day I remember I had grabbed my backpack, filling it with comic books, and all the cookies I could fit. I biked over to the woods and all I did was walk around. For hours I explored every inch of that woods. It was the most...the happiest moment in my life. I've never had any other moment like that one. I remember always wanting to find something extraordinary there, to explore that place like it was the woods of a dangerous murderer or something like that. Of course, this was all before I knew what a murderer really did. The point is, that place, and that day was something that I will never forget. Nothing after that was ever the same. Nothing after that day was simple anymore. Being a kid is the greatest point in anyone's life, and yet it's the shortest point of anyone's life."

(Pause)

"There was only one thing about that day that went wrong, and that's why it sticks in my head so vividly. There was this thin trail within the woods that led down to this tiny creek. It was always my favorite spot to go in the woods. I mean, when you're a kid and you have an opportunity to jump around in a creek, who doesn't want to do that? But that day, there was…this deer that was hurt. And it was just lying there in the grass, inches away from the creek. I remember not wanting to get close because all I could think was that I would scare it and it would run away. But this deer wasn't going to run away.

"A huge gash ran all along the deer's stomach. And there was…all this blood that was dried on the grass, and on the deer's fur. The blood seemed to be everywhere to the little kid in me. I remember thinking that if only the deer were closer to the water, it could wash all the blood away. I sat there for hours and… I watched the deer die. What kind of sick kid does that? I just sat there, doing nothing but staring. The sun came out during the time I was watching it. And it made the blood glisten for a few instances. And for some reason, all I could think of was how pretty the red color looked. Who would even think that? Red is ugly; it's stern and it's harsh… I watched that deer till it died, and then I biked home as if nothing happened.

"When I walked into the house, my mom was on the phone and she was crying. It was the first time I had seen her cry. Her sister had just died in a car crash. She died instantly; no one could have done anything. I had myself convinced that the deer was the reason she was in the accident, even though she lived miles and miles away. I only saw my aunt twice my whole life, and both times there was this emptiness in her eyes that I didn't understand when I was little. I know now that she was so sad about something, I just didn't know. As I got older, I realized that the deer held this same sadness, until about a minute or so before dying. And then there was brightness in its eyes, as if death really was that sweet release. My only hope was that my aunt's eyes held that look when she died, so that all the sadness would be gone."

(Pause)

"Nothing after that day was the same for me. All the innocence in life was taken away. I remember wondering why I couldn't see my aunt again, and missing her even though I barely knew her. And my cousin, she was so mad at me because I wasn't crying at the funeral. But...I didn't know what crying would have even done, besides make me sad and feel sick to my stomach like I always did when I cried. Sometimes I wish I was still as ignorant as when I was little. That everything around me was exactly what it looked like, nothing hidden or mysterious about it. But it's never going to be like that."

"Dan, life doesn't have to be viewed with such a negative aspect. Even with death, there still is happiness within the world."

"But is there? That's what people want to believe and that's what they force themselves to believe, but is it true? When you're little, every memory is happy. Every single thing you did made you feel on top of the world. But once that harsh reality breaks through the mold of imagination, it's all gone. Sure, there are great things that happen in this world, but they seem to always be overshadowed by darker events. Even just the notion of finishing school and starting a job yields with it all sorts of fears, knowing that you have to work on your own, that at any point you could lose everything. That you could be alone..."

(Pause)

"Dan, if it's your future and loneliness that you're frightened of…"

"It's not that at all. I'm frightened of how I'll view the world now that I've seen what I've seen."

(Pause)

"And what was that Dan? What did you see? What happened?"

(Pause)

"Someone died."

# VI

The first night came and went. Dan couldn't even begin to count the number of hours he lay in his bed filling his head with thoughts of nothing and absolutely everything. His mind went from the desire to be back at school, away from the suffocating feeling of home, where questions of current affairs never ceased, to calling Jamie, and to curling up even further within the covers and never moving again. Then there were the hours were he could stare at anything, the window, where the sun slowly began to peak through as the minutes passed, to the calming posters of abstract designs that hung throughout his room, and nothing at all could be produced in his mind. He went through the stages of exhaustion, where his body barely moved the sheets underneath him an inch, to the point where he wanted to move but his body felt like dense lead and then suddenly yearned to be moving.

Regardless, he had quickly exited to the car upon arriving at his house, scrambled up the stairs to his room, and shut himself out from the world. His bags were thrown carelessly against the wall, and immediately he changed to a pair of shorts, his worn clothes from the day clinging to his body in a new layer of sweat. He climbed into the bed, throwing the sheets over, submerging completely into the dark covers. His heart was racing, his mind like an overcharged machine that couldn't slow down. *Calm down Dan, just calm down. It's all a dream, it's not real.* But no amount of encouragement from his mind could take the images away, or stop his body from being wracked with guilt. His mind kept moving a million miles a minute. *Just STOP!!!*

He held his breath. His lungs filled with air, and then became still. His eyes stared directly up at the stark white ceiling above his head. His head began to ache, but still his chest didn't fall. His eyes roamed the ceiling, his head began to bang uncontrollably and his body tingling. A pressure compressed down onto his chest and Dan closed his eyes and slowly let the breath escape him. His chest sank down, his fingers slipping further and further beneath the covers. The pressure slowly ebbed away and with it all the thoughts drew out of Dan's mind. The world was still.

The clock clearly read that it was two in the afternoon. Dan didn't even care. It posed no threat to him. It gave him no worry. There was no demand out there for him, and it was here, in his bland, dark room that Dan finally felt his entire being relax. It was only for brief moments at a time, but in the room he could escape to nothing. No one could find him here, it was an unbreakable enclosure that kept from facing the world, but also kept the world from coming for him. Hushed laughter snuck through the cracks of the doorway as his sister rushed her feet up the stairs as fast as they could carry her.

"Dan!" she called. Dan didn't even move a muscle, but sat staring up at the ceiling, a position that he hadn't moved from in hours. His mind was sluggish, his body itching to be moving. They conflicted violently with each other every moment or two; but in the end Dan let his mind win, closing off every terrible thought that he knew he could have and letting darkness invade. "Dan!"

"Emily, hush! Dan's still sleeping," his mother's composed voice was a tranquil rush of water that cooled any mounting boiling point.

"But he's been asleep forever," the ability that Dan's sister had to elongating syllables was like nails on a chalkboard to Dan. He threw the blankets further over his head, stifling the conversation which still continued outside his door. Eventually he could hear footsteps traveling back downstairs, and the sharp slam of a door. The entire house filled with silence, and Dan was utterly alone.

This had happened so many times before, but for some

reason this time it was different. To be alone meant that no one could be there to help or could tell you what to do. Every action from henceforth was of his own accord. Though his family would only be gone for a few hours, any action Dan could make suddenly made him feel incredibly vulnerable. His room was suddenly shrinking, encasing Dan as he lay still in his bed. He leaped from the bed, turning the door slowly. Every creak was a thousand times louder than normal, and every step he took placed his feet onto the chilled carpet, as if this was the first time he had stepped forth in this house before.

Dan sauntered down the stairs, his hand running along the railing. The lines in the wood snaked all along the railing, the glaze over the finished wood every so often catching against Dan's fingertips. His mind was still fogged up, trapping his thoughts from the previous days. The staircase opened into the living room and the kitchen. Both were sparkling clean, the work of his mother. Not an object was out of place. The cushions lay perfectly against the couch. Every appliance in the kitchen shinned as if it had just been taken out of the box. Dan felt a wave of temptation to go through the entire house and move just bits and pieces; only to see how long it would take before it drove his mom nuts. Not even a spoon was laid out against the marble counter. One wrong setting and the entire ambience of the house would have been different. Dan loved this house, grew up in it and hoped to one day own a house just like it.

But for now, his mind could only focus on the pristine condition that the house upheld, and the urge to change just one thing so that the house couldn't be photographed for a magazine. It was too cheerful, it was too fake. The real world would never look like the inside of the house, so clean and perfect. The world outside this house would never be able to hold this serene fervor, the immaculate complexion. It was the safest environment that Dan knew and he never wanted to leave it. But it was all a lie.

Though his stomach grumbled unceasingly, nothing within the kitchen suited Dan's hunger. Everything looked too sweet or too rich for his stomach, which had been rolling inside and out with panic for days. His hand finally reached for a soda, though even when he cracked it open and took a sip, he felt that the soda only made his throat dryer. The quiet afternoon seemed to linger on, leaving Dan with a few more hours of daylight after he had avoided the rest with sleep. Dan lumbered over to the living room, plopping down on the leather couch and switching the television on. For the next thirty minutes Dan found himself endlessly flipping through channels, every so often stopping on a nonsensical reality show, or a dark drama with ominous music that filled the entire room for a split second. Dan also realized that he flipped right past the news channels without skipping a beat. *Let them say what they want, it didn't happen.*

A sharp tire squeak outside the enormous living room window made Dan turn, the can held directly to his lips. A black sedan, shadowed windows and all, had pulled up right in front of the window. Dan could barely see anybody within the vehicle. The car still ran with a quiet hum, but remained absolutely still on the side of the road. Dan felt his hands begin to shake, the tangy remains of soda sticking to his gaping mouth. He peered closer, slowly leaning forward. His nose almost touched the glass and he tried to catch a glimpse of the driver. Barely seen, the silhouette of a body suddenly came into view, and the person sitting in the car suddenly cocked his head, directly at window. Directly at Dan.

A gasp escaped his lips and his body flew back a whole two feet, slipping off the couch and onto the floor. The can of soda flew from his hands, the brown liquid splattering across the cream colored carpet. Dan's heart was pounding, sweat pooling along his forehead. *What the fuck, what the fuck?* It was all that Dan could think of as he lay along the carpet. The fear that gripped him wouldn't be quenched until he climbed back over that couch, and looked back out that window.

Dan felt his hands lift him back up, his eyes wildly searching all around him. His body inched closer to the edge of the couch, the soft leather crunching underneath his fingers, which gripped the piece of furniture until the knuckles were white as snow. He crouched low, his chest grazing the leather as he slowly raised his head up to the window. His eyes were still wide with terror as he just reached the top of the couch. The windowpane fogged with his heavy breath, immediately clearing up as he took in a deep breath. The car was gone, driving away in the distance, a cloud of exhaust swirling into the air.

"What the hell?" the audible whisper broke the awful silence, for Dan had drowned out every sound around him but the hum of the car as it had sat beside his yard. The television suddenly sounded like it cranked up to full volume, and Dan quickly grabbed the remote and shut it off. The dark stain across the carpet suddenly caught his eye.

"Shit! Shit!" his feet moved at lightning speed as he ran to the kitchen, grabbing the nearest towel and searching for the bottle of stain remover. Obscenities kept pooling under his breath, unstoppable as Dan felt his whole world around him crashing down. "What is going on? What the hell is wrong with me?" He scrambled back into the living, setting the stain remover into the carpet and fervently began to scrub away at the soda that was soaked through. "She's going to kill me…"

The back door that attached to the garage suddenly creaked open. Dan's head snapped up, his hand lingering over the last half of the soda stain.

"Hello, I'm home," his mom's footsteps clicked against the wood floor of the kitchen, her heels rapping sharply closer and closer towards him. "Dan?" He watched her place bags of groceries on the counter, his body still unwavering from its position on the floor. He was a five year old child who had been caught coloring on the walls; only he was twenty going on twenty one, suffering from a brief panic attack with a spilled soda all along his knees. His mom turned, and instantly concern swept over her face.

"Dan? What happened?"

"It was an accident. I'm sorry," he mumbled the words,

feeling ashamed that he not only spilled the soda, but that he consequently felt as bad as he did.

"Oh hon, it's okay. It's just…Dan what happened?" Dan still stared up at his mom, who now dropped to his level, taking the towel from him and circling away at the stain. He stared down as the spots disappeared with a gentle glide of her hand. What would have taken him minutes to fix took her an effortless moment or two. It was graceful, almost beautiful to watch how carefully she padded the carpet, how diligently but without anger she cleaned the mess that she hadn't even made. Just as quickly as he had made the mess, it suddenly was gone. "You can't stay quiet forever, you know that." She was walking back to the kitchen and Dan in appropriate fashion followed her in. She placed the towel and the bottle away, turning around with a hand on her hip, leaning against the counter.

"There uh…there was this car that parked in front of our yard and…I could have sworn the guy was scoping me out. I freaked out, I guess. And now that I've said that it sounds really dumb. I'm sorry Mom." A wave of heat washed over Dan as he looked stupidly down at his feet, his toes picking away at the wood below. His mom's eyes roamed his entire face, her gentle eyes that only wanted to hug him, but she knew deep down inside that there was something more stirring within her son that a well-gestured hug couldn't fix.

"Dan, is everything alright? And I'm not just talking about right now. Is everything alright with school and everything?"

*I'm the only one who thinks I'm going crazy. How's that for starters?* He wanted to tell her everything. Was it even possible to tell her everything? He knew that once he started, he would only get so far before she would stop him, say he was wrong and try to make everything right. But this wrong was never going to be fixed. His eyes belied the whole truth, but so did his mom's. He had never seen true worry in his mom's eyes before this moment. She knew that he was hiding something; she knew that he wanted nothing more than to scream and shout everything that was going on inside his head. But instead, he felt a different set of words come out of his mouth than what was expected from both of them. There was no trust, and a barrier and suddenly been built up between them in a blink of an eye.

"Yeah, just stressed from school. You know, all the homework and stuff. I'll be fine. I just need another few days of sleep."

His family barely talked to him that night. His mom gave nothing but short, curt answers, and then, by the end of the night she acted as if nothing was wrong. His sister called him annoying because he wouldn't say much and promptly stood up from the couch and ran upstairs to dutifully slam the door like every well-bred teenager. His dad said only a few things, asked a few basic questions and then lumbered off to bed, claiming that he was exhausted from work. The movie began and ended with barely any words spoken, and Dan's mom only provided a quick good night and a brush against his shoulder before going to bed. Dan was once again alone in the dimly illuminated living room, which to Dan seemed to stretch too far up, and contained too many dark corners.

The sounds of the night could be heard, the chirps of animals and birds, the snaps and creaks of tree branches whacking up against each other, and every once in a while there was the faint sound of a car driving by. Every brake light and every metallic sound that emanated from a car made Dan pause, his eyes glancing back over to the huge bay window and outside. The black of night engulfed the whole night, but he still felt something there. The floor above him creaked as his sister left her room and walked towards the bathroom. Dan held his breath and waited for her to go back to her room.

Minutes passed with no sound. But then, within the dark hallway that led to the backyard, Dan heard a faint whisper, calling his name. *So I really am insane,* he felt himself nonchalantly think. *Damn.*

"Dan, I need you to explain to me what happened and what you saw."

"I don't want to talk about it."

"That's not an option now Dan. You just confessed to me—"

"Confessed, confessed? You make it seem like I did it!"

"Dan, that is hardly the message I'm trying to get across. However, you still need to tell me what you saw."

"I saw a girl get murdered! I turned the corner and watched a girl get hacked to death. Roman Polanski and I could have a fucking good conversation right now. We could compare how it was done and what the body looked like afterwards and everything! I saw a person die, and I just sat there!"

"When did this happen?"

"It felt like it was a dream. I don't even remember that night. I remember being so exhausted I thought I could collapse anywhere and sleep for days. I don't even remember walking home that night or seeing it happen. It was all a dream, I swear."

"Dan, would you consider yourself an insomniac?"

"It's college, everyone's an insomniac."

"Dan."

"What!"

"Have you told anyone about what you saw? Did you call the police?"

"No."

"Dan, the police need to know about this."

"They already do, the body's already gone. I can guarantee that a nice funeral was given and everything. They even tried to clean the wall." (Laughs) "You can see where the bleach and the soap and every other chemical that could possibly wipe away blood are along the wall. But the blood still stains right through it. That much blood shouldn't come out of a body."

"Dan, would you want to talk to the police? Tell them what you saw."

(Pause)

"No."

"Why not?"

(Pause)

"The worst part is there's no one else to blame but myself."

"Why do you say that?"

"Because…for those brief moments that girl's life was in my hands…and then I let it happen."

"You don't know that you could have stopped them. They could have killed you too Dan."

(Pause)

"I could have tried…to stop them…"

"Dan…"

"Are you going to call the cops on me? I didn't even see the guy's faces. I couldn't tell them which suspect they should be looking for, I swear to god!"

"Dan! Calm down. I won't call the cops unless I feel that it is impeding on your safety."

(Pause)

"I feel like that's breaking some major rule that you should be following as a doctor."

"We don't need to discuss that right now Dan."

(Pause)

"Do you remember hearing about that girl in the sixties, who was murdered and a ton of people just sat there and watched?"

"I do actually. Her name was Kitty Genovese."

"How old were you when that happened?"

"I was ten."

"Do you remember what you thought when you heard that people were there on the scene but didn't stop it from happening?"

(Sigh)

"Dan, I was ten, it doesn't matter—"

"Just answer the question."

(Pause)

"I remember thinking that if I was there, I would have stopped them. And that was all my ten year old mind could think of."

"Huh...funny how a child's mind can be stronger than an adult's. Wasn't that whole innocent bystander studied and given a title?

"It's called the Genovese Syndrome. It's the idea that bystanders watch something horrible, like a murder occur, and there's diffusion in social responsibility. It's mainly due to the idea that people don't want to be hurt like that victim is. It's a natural and completely understandable thought process. People want to live, that's why they try to prolong life as much as possible."

(Pause)

"Well, I definitely have Genovese Syndrome. Lucky me."

"Dan, I would like to schedule more appointments with you. I feel that we should be discussing this a lot more."

"I don't want to talk about it anymore."

"Dan, I feel that it is important we talk about this and help you through it. This is a very traumatic thing to witness."

(Pause)

"We don't need to. By spring it won't matter."

# VII

The reluctance to go back to school had Dan hanging onto every minute longer that he could spend at home. The last afternoon he jumped at every opportunity that his mom gave him to run an errand. A quick car ride with his sister suddenly turned into an excursion after he dropped her off at the high school. Without any sort of visible emotion, Dan found himself quickly veering towards the coast, driving closer and closer to the only spot that calmed him.

The roads twisted and curved; a black vein that ran across the green skin of the earth around him. Every so often a line of trees reached their way towards the sky, and houses sat in shadowed light as clouds swam across the blue ocean of the sky. The music was up to full volume, the windows were rolled down, and Dan aimlessly and recklessly found himself driving on the streets. Not even the thought of being pulled over, tormented by cops for speeding, slowed him down, but rather propelled him faster. The only thought that drew through his mind was the need, the desire to be utterly and fully alone.

A gravel path veered to the left and Dan's car swerved directly towards, kicking up dust and rocks as he disappeared from the populated highway. The path became narrower, a secret trail leading towards the ocean. It was a sacred spot for Dan, one that he hoped no one but he would ever find.

The distant crash of waves and the pungent smell of the salt from the sea suddenly exploded into Dan's senses. The car slowed and eventually came to a halt. Dan climbed out of the car, taking off his shoes and haphazardly abandoning them next to his parked car.

The sand immediately sucked his toes further into the ground, the warmth from the sun seeping into his dry skin. He took quick steps forward, anxiously wishing to view the blue sea. Gulps of air entered his lungs as Dan felt himself take the deepest breaths he could take, unwilling to give up this last moment of freedom.

The sea. It was dangerous, it was peaceful, and it was infinite. The waves that crashed against the sand were small, but they still issued out a foam-filled roar before barging into the soft ground. The long grass around Dan swayed in the breeze, cattails itching to pop, the last of the summer critters fluttering around the green tendrils that hung down like spiny fingers. The sun peeked in and out of clouds, filling the earth with quick warmth before being hindered by the gathering gray clouds.

Dan closed his eyes, watching the red sun beneath his eyelids turn to a dark black as the clouds overtook the entire ocean view around him. His eyes snapped open, every part of his body alert. His fingertips tingled as he grazed them along the sand. The waves still came up to the sand before becoming hesitant and floating back into the ocean. Weariness hung in the air as the waters suddenly went from blue to a dull, lifeless gray.

"I could walk into the sea right now...I could walk in and no one would notice me...no one would see." It was an airy whisper, spoken by a confused voice. Dan stood up, withdrawing from his pockets his cell phone, keys, and wallet, discarding them into the soft sand. His toes wrapped themselves into the sand below him, curling the grains of glass and left over rock deep within his skin, embedding it all underneath his feet.

Assuredly, his body began to move closer. His feet took giant strides and soon Dan felt the cool water brush along his feet. The water washed up all around, gliding against his skin and sinking back into the ocean again. Dan walked deeper and deeper, feeling the freezing cold water mix with the warmer air; a mixture that sent his body into waves of turmoil. His legs froze while his brow gained sweat from the heat. His chest was soon immersed into the water, his shirt clinging to his body and dragging him further in. His fingers slid into the water, his arms rapidly following suit.

"No one would even know."

His head was submerged. The beads of water that surrounded his face were tiny icicles that bit into his skin; ravenous parasites that only wanted to break in and infect his whole body. His arms hung weightless at his sides, his fingers still pushing through the water as he forced his body to not bob back up. The ocean suddenly turned a deep blue and Dan's eyes turned up towards the surface. The blurred sky hanging above him was a bright, unbelievable blue. The smeared portrait of the sky shimmered as the sun began fracturing the water, cutting deep wounds into the ocean as spears of light appeared all around Dan. Bubbles pooled at his lips and swam upwards towards the sky.

And then his toes became numb. His skin around his fingers shriveled as the feeling left them. His eyesight became filled with bright sports, red and orange and blue, all intermingling together as the sun once again faded from view. His lungs tightened, begging for air. He still ever so slightly moved his arms, pushing his body back to the ocean ground, his feet brushing against smooth stones weathered from age. His head lolled back, his lungs tightened more and his legs became seized stumps hooked to his body.

Dan felt a black smoke peek into the sides of his vision. He closed his eyes, opened them, but the darkness was still there. The entire time, all Dan thought of were his precise movements: the way he felt his fingers curl, his toes sway, and his hair dance with the current. It was all so simple, movements that humans involuntarily do every day. And yet here he was, voluntary stopping movements, while voluntary embracing other gestures that he never realized were so amazing before. Suddenly realizing that one's fingers curl into a fist, or spread out into a wave became the most fascinating thing to Dan.

And then it was all of their faces. That's what entered Dan's mind next. It was his family, his friends. It was Jamie's face, with her bright eyes. It was her face, with her stained red skin; the skin that Dan knew underneath the bloodshed would be a perfect alabaster. His eyes burned relentlessly from the ocean, a flickering lightshow blurring the faces that were stuck in his mind. His arms suddenly sprung to life. His legs kicked up the ground beneath him, a cloud of sand swirling around his legs. The darkening sky drew closer and Dan's head suddenly burst through the clear shell of the ocean. The warm air reignited his whole body as it sprung back from its frozen state. His lungs expanded, filling with as much as Dan could take in. His eyesight still sparkled with lights, but soon faded away and brought Dan back to reality. He bobbed in the water, feeling his toes suddenly wriggle free with vivaciousness and his legs effortlessly kick him back towards the shore. He placed one leg in front of him, and felt it crumble under the weight of the rest his body, catching himself with his hands; he finally pushed himself back up right.

The ocean suddenly was smaller than what he remembered. The feet of water soon became inches, and he was a Goliath towering over a small pool of water. Dan turned and looked back out. The ocean was suddenly a monster, a rapacious beast that could swallow him whole. He looked back down at his feet and the ocean was suddenly small again, a tiny world that he could crush with a single step. He took his feet completely out of the water and looked back at all that surrounded him. The world was a hellish gray and Dan felt with every fiber in his being that he suddenly hated this place. It was a demanding partner that never gave anything back in return. Countless hours that Dan spent in the presence of the ocean only left Dan in a somber mood. The ocean couldn't even provide a form of sustenance, the salty taste that Dan licked off his lips causing his empty stomach to roll in disagreement. He grabbed his belongings, walked back up to his car, and drove off.

His mom didn't say a word when her son walked into the house with his hair and clothes still damp. A polite exchange of words and his bags were packed up into the car and they began the trip back to school. His mother didn't pry and Dan barely spoke at all, his head leaning against the glass and his eyes scanning the world as he sharply passed it by along the highway. The sky grew darker, suddenly gushed with enormous amounts of rain on the car. Dan followed the raindrops as they dribbled down the crystal clear glass window. The streetlights and the buzz of life suddenly began to appear as he and his mom drove past groups of students.

"You make sure to call if you need anything." It was not a statement but rather a question that escaped his mom's lips. Dan turned towards her. Her face was calm, her cheekbones clenched as she tried to appear strong, but Dan saw in her eyes the constant worry that had grown from the scene in the living room the other day.

"I will, Mom; don't worry." A small smile tugged her lips and she leaned towards Dan, hugging him with an endearment that neither could ignore. "Be safe driving home Mom."

"I will. Love you, Dan."

"Love you too, Mom." He climbed out of the car and grabbed his bags, wishing to be free from the scene; for he knew that once she began to drive away, he'd want nothing more than to go back home and stay there.

Stepping along the cracked steps of the apartment's entryway, Dan begrudgingly made his way back to his apartment. The lock clicked and he sauntered in, throwing his stuff in his room. A door creaked open and his roommate yawned as he rubbed the back of his head, heading straight for the kitchen and grabbing a cup to fill with ice water.

"Dude, how was your break? You're getting in late," he remarked. Dan tossed his wallet on his dresser; checking his phone, which was empty, and then slipping it back into his pants pocket.

"Yeah, decided to stay for the extra meal. It was fine though, slept a lot." He walked back into the quiet living room, flopping down on the couch and turning the television on.

"I hear that, gotta love the free food. Oh hey—" His

roommate's head popped around the corner of the kitchen wall. "A cop called the other day. Said that he wanted to speak with you. What the hell have you been doing that a cop wants to speak with you?" His head had already disappeared when asking the last question, hiding Dan's stunned face and rigid body from view.

"Don't have a clue."

(Phone ringing, clicking to voicemail)

"Hey Jamie…it's…it's Dan. I know I'm calling really late; it's like 2 am. I swear I'm not drunk. I just…I guess I just wanted to talk. I haven't been able to hang with you in a bit, which sucks and…I don't even know why I called, really. How was your break by the way? Wow, that sounds completely stupid and idiotic now that I've said it. Haven't seen you in the last couple of lectures by the way…"

(Pause)

"I…I'm so sorry for calling you this late. It won't happen again. Just, if you don't mind, give me a call back…. bye."

(Hangs up phone)

"How have you been, Dan?"

(Silence)

"Shrugging your shoulders really doesn't suffice as an answer."

"I don't know, I'm back at school, there's homework again. Same old shit."

"I meant, how are you doing with…well with what we discussed last time we met?"

"Fine."

"Just fine."

"Just fine. I've been trying to not think about it anymore."

(Pause)

"I see. How well have you been sleeping?"

(Pause)

"Why do you ask?"

"Well, you look exhausted, Dan. And as these sessions continue I see that you've become increasingly more and more tired looking. You've lost weight. You barely talk at our sessions anymore, whereas when you first started you were very open with your opinions and now you've closed yourself off completely it seems."

(Pause)

"Well, I guess I've hit a rut."

"Good to see your humor hasn't been wasted."

"Has anyone ever told you that you're an ass?"

(Chuckles)

"Plenty of people, actually. Of course, many of those people also realized that I helped them in many ways.

"Well, aren't you just the epitome of perfection."

"I don't want to have to fight past your sarcasm. Are you unhappy with me?"

"How can you really be so sure of yourself? I mean, you're dripping with narcissism and a cool attitude as you diagnose my thoughts day after day. What if after all this I was just playing you, and you were wrong?"

"That'd be a mighty heavy con Dan."

"Yeah, that'd be an awesome con, wouldn't it?"

(Pause)

"Have you talked to Jamie recently?"

"Why does it matter?"

"Why did you suddenly get defensive?"

(Pause)

"No, I haven't."

"Why not?"

"She hasn't been at school. I've tried calling her, but she doesn't answer and she's not at lectures anymore."

"Do you think something happened to her?"

"I dunno."

"Perhaps she ended up leaving the school?"

(Silence)

"Are you not concerned with her disappearance at all?"

"Not really. Maybe she's ignoring my calls. Maybe she took a trip and extended her break. Who the hell cares?"

"I was just asking Dan."

"Well, thanks for asking. At least I know that you're concerned about me."

"As my patient, yes, I am."

(Pause)

"Have you told your parents yet?"

"Told them what, about Jamie?"

"About the murder."

"No."

"I still feel that I should urge you to tell your parents."

"Good thing you can't control minds then, isn't Doc?"

"Dan—"

"I said I don't want to talk about it and I wasn't lying. I want to try and forget it."

"This isn't something that can be easily forgotten. This is something that can haunt a person. Do you still see her face Dan? Do you still envision every single moment of that night?"

(Silence)

"Dan?"

"So what if I do?"

"Dan, what did you mean when you said in our last session that by spring it won't matter?"

"What?"

"You said by spring none of this is going to matter. Why?"

"Cause it won't. It'll be enough time that I'll forget it even happened."

"Do you think it'll be that easy, that you can just forget anything ever happened?"

"Why not?"

"That's not how the human mind works Dan. A brain builds up memories for a reason."

"Well, not this brain."

"Dan—"

"Can we please just drop this?"

"I want to start individual sessions."

"What the hell does that mean? This is individual right now. You and me, that's it."

"I want you to start having sessions by yourself. These sessions would be in single rooms; just a tape recorder and you are free to say whatever comes to mind."

"Aren't I allowed to do that here?"

"Dan, we both know that bias thoughts come into play. My

reactions can drastically change your thoughts, as well as how well you open up."

"And an inanimate object is going to change that? Great faith you have in humanity!"

"Dan, I feel that these sessions would be good. You can say whatever is on your mind and no one will be there to interrupt—"

"Will you listen to them after?"

"Dan…"

"Will you listen to them after?"

"Of course I will."

"Then it doesn't make it different at all. In fact it makes it feel like an even greater invasion of privacy."

"Dan, I feel like with the situation you have faced that it would best to include the sessions for yourself."

"Well that's great, but you didn't face the situation. You have no idea what's going on in my head? You don't know my thoughts, you don't need to know them and frankly, I doubt I'd say anymore to those stupid tapes than I'd say to your face!"

"Dan, as your doctor—"

"As my doctor you can say whatever the fuck you want, doesn't mean I have to listen!

"Your right Dan, you don't have to listen. You can wallow in your thoughts, you can tear your mind apart until the last inch of you doesn't care whether or alive or not, cause you'll be pooling in your own dark, scary thoughts. Or, you can trust me and let me help you. I'm here to help you Dan, help you through what you've been through—"

"You don't even understand what I've been through! You've never witnessed what I have!"

"Maybe you're right Dan! But if you'd open up to me and tell me what is going on, then I could understand and then I could help! Forgive me for not being the doctor that has witnessed every horrific thing in the world, but my job is to treat patients that have witness those things, and my job is to help them realize that there is a life still worth living for!"

(Silence)

"This would be so much easier if this were just one big, long con. Then I could walk out of here with a smile on my face, chuckling with glee. Instead, I walk out pissed off. Still wonder why I think you're an ass? Cause this whole conversation gives me a pretty big clue. Why don't you listen to it again when I leave, cause I know you will, and call me with your thoughts on forcing me to do something I don't want. You might even have the same opinion as me for once. How about that?"

(Silence)

"I'm not speaking out loud for a lousy tape recorder. Fuck that."

# VIII

Dan didn't call the cop back. His number was written on a yellow post-it, stuck to the fridge. Every single time he reached for the fridge door, he stared at the number. In fact, he had memorized the number. It was burned into his brain; seven tiny digits that held such weight that often times he felt those numbers replace every other thought in his mind. His house number suddenly was the cop's number. Every black car that pulled up in front of his apartment was the cop, surreptitiously glancing up to Dan's window, looking for any traces of the boy. Dan kept low; quiet for reasons he couldn't even explain. He barely left his apartment unless it struck him that he should finally return to his lectures. But once stepping forth into the class, feeling the beady eyes of everyone on him, he clamped up and stayed silent. His professors would look at him with weary eyes, but ultimately brush it aside as just another student that barely slept and instead stayed out for late nights and boozed memories. No one considered that Dan inside was cracking at the seams, a fragile being that at any point could suddenly break and lose all sense of reality around him.

The air around him became satiated with worry. His roommates gave him awkward glances as they watched him trudge out of his room, eyes glazed with exhaustion that had yet to be quenched. Conversations about nothing and yet everything had turned into small quips at one another. Dan barely said a word, and his roommates couldn't decide whether it was a growing demise towards them, or because there was something deep seeded with Dan that they hadn't a clue on how to deal with. So instead they fluttered around the apartment, talking about unnecessary things, and assuming that since he answered, Dan was doing well.

His mother did little to help. Without speaking about the incident on his last day home, her voice still was stinging with remorse and guilt, as if her constant love and devotion was what was causing Dan to become more guarded. The scene replayed again and again in her head. Her soaked sun simply setting his keys down on the kitchen counter, looking at her with cold eyes, and then drifting up to his room. She stared at the keys for minutes afterward, listening for signs of life from the upstairs bedroom, contemplating whether or not to speak up. Instead she too remained silent, and now her choice racked her brain every day. She should have talked to him, asked him again if everything was okay. But he assuredly came downstairs moments later, saying that he had driven to the beach and was now packed and ready to go. His eyes had dimmed down a little from the icy stare that they had held earlier, only now they looked drained and worn out.

Dan felt the same upon arriving back at school. Every little thing he did seemed to be a burden, every task a constant burden. Though he hadn't fallen behind and couldn't care less about the status of his schoolwork, Dan felt that the daily chore of reading and writing and studying would never end. He would sit at his desk and stare, wondering what the point of all this studying was, should he even care and would the next page of text be as boring as the first. He tried his best to ignore the girl, the image of her slipping to the ground, of her being drained dry. He strategically crossed the other side of the street, and always made a point to look at something else when the alleyway came into view, or busy himself with his phone. Numerous conversations with his mother suddenly occurred while he was walking back to his apartment. She dimwittedly assumed that this was when her son was free; when in reality he was too afraid to be alone by himself and this place.

There was only one sure thing that had steadied him, keeping him from losing control over the thoughts that agonized his mind.

Jamie had finally called back, after an anxious week of her missing from class and showing no sign that she even existed. Her voice when she called was perky, but still extra sensitive. They played the role of small talk, simple words asking how the other was doing.

Finally Dan felt himself blurting out that he'd like to see her, and with a sense of hesitance, Jamie agreed. Though they spoke rarely in lecture, Jamie suddenly was appearing more and more around the apartment. She and Dan would start the conversation about class, a classic innocence that both of them felt the need to break within minutes. Suddenly the conversation would turn to how Jamie had disappeared for a week or so, which she still had to divulge to Dan.

"What is this, twenty questions?"

"No, I just, was curious where you were. You didn't come to lecture for days." She could always pause before giving a coy smile at Dan.

"Guess I just wanted to take an extended vacation." Dan felt himself crumble with unease under her smile, but still itched to be closer to her. The tables always turned onto him though, as Jamie brutishly remarked on Dan's pale complexion, the growing bags under his eyes and the shrunken figure.

"Do you eat?" Dan scuffs.

"I'd be dead now if I didn't eat."

"Well then do you sleep? You look like the walking dead!" Dan would always give a feeble attempt to change the subject, but the scrutiny that he received from Jamie showed him that she knew he was hidden something, and ever so devilishly was trying to coax it out of him.

"I guess I've been having trouble sleeping. I'm probably an insomniac."

"Trouble falling asleep, staying asleep, barely eating and functioning when you are awake? Oh yeah, definitely an insomniac." Any other person she could have talked to would have shunned Jamie's cynical air, but to Dan it was a comfort that he clung to. He laughed at her cynicism, comparing it to his own ill-ridden humor. A huge part of him felt the urge to tell Jamie what he had seen, but the other part of him instead relished in her presence, and would fight to the end to not screw up the instant friendship that the two had built up over the better part of the semester.

"So, do you think I should call the cop back?" They had been quietly studying on Dan's couch. Numerous books were opened and notebook pages were crinkled and flattened, notes that they both scavenged up in order to study for an upcoming test. Jamie sat cross-legged on the couch, while Dan was fervently flipping through pages and pages of textbook that he had yet to even read. He had stopped when she didn't respond right away, glancing over at her face, which was looking slightly beyond him in thought.

"What do you think it's about?" she asked.

"No idea, kind of figured if it was really important he would have called back."

"Yeah, maybe it's just a parking violation or something, I mean, you've had your car here for a couple weeks right?"

"Yeah, hopefully that's all it is." Jamie looked back down at her notes, withdrawing a highlighter and lining numerous amounts of her notes. Dan felt his head rest on his hand, leaning against the arm of the couch. The words blurred, the lines that he had written from lectures that he hardly paid attention in all came together in one big blur within his vision. Sounds drifted in and out of earshot. A scratch from Jamie's pen was suddenly an earthquake in his mind, while the television that lay only a few feet from him was a soft whisper.

His eyes would close and then snap back open. His head would loll and he could force himself to bring it back up. The heavy weight of the pen in his hand made him rest it at his side and Dan felt himself slip into a fog as his mind finally shut down and his body gave up. Days without sleep took its toll, and Dan felt himself fall into the deepest slumber that he thought possible. Within the minutes, or perhaps hours that he was laying on the couch, he dimly heard Jamie pack up her things, shake him awake and say that she was leaving. He mumbled words, couldn't remember them now, and heard the door quietly click as she said that she'd call him later. The television still droned on, and there was even the croon of the radio as his roommate finally came home, sneaking past Dan into his room.

Dan had the sense that he was still awake. It was a cloudy haze that hung over his eyes, a blindness that covered him. He could hear everything, the radio playing, and the fridge opening as his roommate grabbed food. He could sense that his arm was cold; that the pen dropped from his fingers and that his leg was losing feeling as he fell deeper and deeper into a slumber. His mind was still buzzing and yet was working at a sluggish pace.

The sudden knocks of the door made Dan snap his head up. A breath caught in his throat and he gulped air as fast as he could, his chest heaving. He looked around wildly, disoriented with everything going on. The door continued knocking and Dan sat shaking his head, trying to get rid of the fog. *Is Jamie here? What? Jamie was here, she left. Wait, what?*

Dan numbly stood up, his legs heavy weights that held him down as he tried to get closer and closer to the door. *Who the hell is here?* The door swung open. The cop was tall, and he wore navy. That was all Dan knew. He had to look up to see him, to look him straight in the eye, which he was trying very hard not to do. The man stood like a cop, tall and upright, one hand strapped to his belt and the other on a pad of paper. Dan concentrated on the pad of paper, the badge on the cop's uniform, the metal nametag that gleamed in the light. It was all nerve wracking. Dan felt sweat begin to pool on his forehead. Heat radiated from his head as if to stamp the guilt on his face.

"Can I help you?" Dan's voice was direct, anything but subtle and in fact downright rude. The cop had to glance up from his notes, staring Dan directly in the eye. *Shit, shit, shit, shit!* It was the only word Dan could think of, at the most inappropriate of times.

"Dan Braddock?" The cop had a deep voice, one that made a person cringe underneath its credence, which is exactly what Dan felt himself doing.

"Yeah, is everything alright?" *No, I was not out that night, I was sleeping. No, I have no idea who the girl is and have never seen her in my life. I have to stop sweating, stop sweating! Shut up, just let it go! Stop!* And to top it off, the cop seemed to sit and stare, as if he found amusement in watching Dan squirm under his gaze.

"Is that your car parked across the street?"

What? My car? Shit, my car. Why the hell did I leave here? What the hell is wrong with me?

"Umm, yeah, yeah that's my car." The cop paused, gave Dan a long look and then began scribbling a ticket.

"You've had it parked the past couple of days in a spot that it shouldn't be. It's a violation, pay the ticket, move your car." The paper made a sharp ripping sound and suddenly was being handed to Dan, who gingerly took it while his other hand gripped the door so hard that all the blood rushed out of his hand and became a white case of flesh against the wood.

"Will do, officer." The cop nodded, placing the paper in his back pocket.

"Have a good day Mr. Braddock." The door closed, the paper was folded up and the ticket was shoved into his pocket. A wave crushed over Dan as relief clung to every pore of his body. He slumped against the door as it shut, feeling his knees collapse underneath him and his back slide down the door. He felt his chest tighten and release as it desperately tried to grab for air. His body awkwardly stood back up, his hands reaching for every piece of furniture to stabilize him as he walked over to the window. His fingers drew into the space between the blinds and he slowly pushed them down. The cop exited the apartment complex, strutting towards his car with an air of superiority. Dan peeked through the blinds, the window fogging with his breath and just as quickly clearing back up. The cop's head turned, and took a long stare back up at Dan. Dan's body crumbled, his hand dragging along the blinds as he fell back down to the floor. He knows, he fucking knows.

(Sigh)

"So, I guess I have to do this stupid independent session. Yeah…don't even know where to begin. But lucky for me, Doc left me this questionnaire sheet in order to prompt my thoughts."

"Name? Dan. Wow, big piece of news right there!"

(Pause)

"What do you feel is bothering you? Seriously. What doesn't bother me? I go day after day to class, deal with people who couldn't give a shit about what happens to me, and oh yeah, saw someone get murdered. Now on top of that I can't get to sleep, can't really eat, concentrate on schoolwork, and the cops are after me. Is this the shit you want to hear Doc? Huh?"

(Pause)

"Maybe this isn't all happening, you know? Maybe I'm imagining half this shit. It just…it doesn't seem that way. Everything this semester feels more real than anything I've experienced in my life."

(Chuckles)

"What kills me is that people crave a life like this: living on the edge, in constant fear and worry. People say it gets them off, gives them a thrill. Didn't know living everyday wishing someone would confront you, yet wishing that no one would see you at all could be so thrilling. What's so great about what I saw? Do people really want to see that, be haunted by it? What they show in movies, or on TV; yeah that shit looks very real sometimes, but you can still tell yourself that it's all fake. That the actor ate a lot of blood colored chocolate that day in order to look like he was choking to death. But the truth is, none of that's real. No matter how much you want it to be. You can always turn the TV off or walk out of the movie theater if it's too much and go back to the ideal life that you always have wanted deep down inside. One night of thrills that doesn't really exist, and you're fulfilled for a bit. And they say I have the screwed up mind. Next question.

"What's your biggest fear?"

(Pause)

"You know how adults grow up and suddenly become all nostalgic about their younger life. As if the younger life was suddenly so much better than the life they live now?"

(Pause)

"My life isn't going to be like that. Cause if I make it past all of this shit, I'm not going to be nostalgic when I'm forty, remembering the good old days when I was twenty and could do anything. Cause here I am, and I've got nothing to show for it. There's nothing that's worth remembering, and there's certainly nothing to be wistful about. If I make it forty I'll be lucky."

(Pause)

"I don't want to be alone, but I know I will be. I'm not cut out to find someone, get married, and have kids. How am I supposed to explain to my kids that I watched someone get murdered and didn't do anything about it? It's like trying to explain to them there's no Santa Claus. I could scar them for life."

(Chuckles)

"I can't believe I just compared Santa Claus to a girl getting murdered. What the hell is wrong with me?"

(Pause)

"Doc keeps asking me why I don't tell anyone, and frankly I don't even know anymore. I feel like if I told someone I'd be able to get help; but yet I want to be selfish in my own right. No matter what I saw, how I describe it, no one is going to understand what any of this means to be. Only I get it. Maybe that's why I haven't said anything. Plus, does it even matter at this point? It's not like I did it, I can't get in trouble for it. Can I?"

(Pause)

"Ummm…"

(Pause)

"Yeah, I really don't want to go through this questionnaire shit anymore. Guess I still have twenty minutes to kill. So, Doc, what have you deciphered so far? Have I opened up to you yet?"

(Pause)

"I know that you'll really want to know this, I started hanging out with Jamie again. She was gone for a bit because…well…I actually don't know why she was gone. She won't tell me. She actually doesn't really say much about herself at all; she normally just lets me talk about my shit before she does. Hey, guess she's kind of like you. Only better cause I don't have to deal with all your snide remarks when I'm talking to her.

"It's been really nice though. I've realized that I'm not afraid to tell her a lot about me. I'm not as closed off. I haven't told her about the girl, but I'm thinking I might soon…"

(Pause)

"I can't even think straight anymore. Jesus, I'm so tired. I'm sick of trying so hard at all this shit! It's all too much!"

(Pause)

"I just…I want to be done with it all…"

(Pause)

"Yeah, that's about all you're going to get from me Doc. I'm out. This is bullshit."

# IX

To say that Dan wanted to be done with school was a gross understatement. It had become exceedingly impossible for him to accomplish the daily routine that everyday life had placed on him. Nights were spent locked in his room, shutting out every inch of light. His body complained of exhaustion, yet his mind still roamed free. His eyes would only stare straight up, towards the gray ceiling. Slowly but surely over the course of the night, Dan found himself tracing the grooves of the ceiling above him. Lines and cracks became pathways for the endless path that he drew. The small, tiny dimples of the ceiling from where paint had either clumped or been brushed unevenly bubbled alive at night, entertaining Dan's acute awareness as he lay in bed until the sunlight appeared.

Extinguishing every form of light, even going so far as to covering the window with a thick blanket, quenched the shadows and shapes. But even still, Dan felt his eyes close ever so slightly for a second, and then snap open. The dread that covered his entire body, making it a rigid casing over his mind and heart, would cause him to sit up and search for something that was never there. The clock next to him ticked, knocking away the tiny minutes that yielded the old day with the new one. It was a mocking clock, which would never move faster when Dan willed it to, but rather slowed down to an unbearable pace. But when Dan yearned for the sleep most, when he finally felt his body quiver into relaxation and his mind finally drain of every thought that was in his head, that's when the clock suddenly sprang to life.

Classes, which many could have viewed to be the savior in

the pitiful hole that Dan had dug himself in, became only a second demon to his wandering mind. Instead of focusing on the continuous murmur that protruded from his professors' lips, Dan's eyes and ears were on every movement around him. The slightest glance from another person in the lecture hall suddenly made Dan's back inflexible, a stiff board that mimicked the harsh plastic seat behind him. Even moments after the person had completely forgotten the position Dan was sitting in, where his hands and feet were placed, and how his facial features were coming more and more defined with hardness; Dan still felt their eyes. He squirmed, he coughed, and he yawned, any action that could make the feeling go away.

But it still crept up to him, a slithering spider that no one notices in the classroom but that one person. It was the feeling that if he took a step outside of the doorway, another person would be asking him what he was doing that night. Was he drunk, was he high on drugs? *No, I was studying!* Was he really though? The conflicting images of him sleeping soundly in his bed to his roommate giving him the first of many perplexed looks made him rake his brain for any indication that it all was still a dream, in which he really didn't walk past the ghastly scene. But no matter how hard he tried to convince himself it didn't happen, the red wall that he was always forced to talk past begged to differ.

The time that ticked away in class lectures only made his sickening mind more diseased with thoughts and feelings that he tried to banish away. Notebook pages were filled with doodles, random notes that he finally paid attention to and snippets of quotes that only he knew what the connotation contained. And strangely enough though, his eyes always trailed back to the windows. Dan became immersed in watching the people who traveled back and forth across campus. What became unnerving though was he always found that one person who seemed to glance over and then never look away. The calm setting that a window should yield, a beautiful canvas to the outside world, had become a torture chamber that enclosed Dan and made him recede back into the panicked thoughts of his mind. He knew deep down that the person had probably walked away, that they couldn't possibly see him through the thick glass that separated them feet away from each other. But nevertheless, a sweat would suddenly drench him, terror would grip him, and he felt himself unable to focus or calm down. That, combined with the outstanding fear that he would be cornered outside the doorway, made minutes pass before Dan would even consider leaving the classroom feeling safe.

An impromptu visit home seemed to be the only thing Dan could think of to help him forget about school. The desire to pack up everything he owned and bring it all back home without a second glance crossed his mind multiple times. Dan felt however, that a piece of him was always going to be stuck at school, and for whatever reason it was, whether it terrified or delighted him, it would always cause him to eventually turn the car around and drive back. For now, it was a quick reprieve back to the home that brought security to every moment in his life thus far that made Dan climb into his car after a tiring week of class and begin the trek to his family.

It had been dark all day, with growing gray clouds and gusts of wind that tore at every feeble little item in the street and brought it with on its invisible path. When Dan finally climbed into his car and drove off, the sky was a threatening barrier that clashed harshly against the calm and restful campus. The air had gradually become colder and colder, making the entire world feel brisk and sharp. It was the undying presence of autumn soon freezing into winter that lingered in the air. Even though, Dan peeked up through his window to the dark cloud above him. The hint of tiny flakes wanted to burst forth and melt against the dying grass was apparent, but they were not yet set free and instead danced an icy waltz up in the clouds.

The thick highway was soon drenched in darkness as Dan drove further and further away from the dense city and suburbs into the quiet, forlorn areas where only few houses could be seen, and quiet neighborhoods were set deep into the growth of the earth. Not even the sound of cars or traffic could break the quiet serenity of the area around Dan. It was a happy place for happy people. It wasn't the average living area where at least one family was the black sheep, or a neighborhood that once one crossed the train tracks was the neighborhood that one had to ban their kids from. It was a lustrous suburb in which people could live the perfect life: The American Dream. And Dan felt more out of place than ever as he drove back towards it.

Tiny raindrops had begun to gather on the windshield, slowly sliding down the thick glass and leaving a trail of moisture all along the way. Dan clicked his wipers on, the cheap plastic swiping away the water and groaning in pain as they wiped newly dried glass, squeaking back to their original positions. The rain though soon came in sheets, and Dan looked around in amazement to find that his headlights were the only ones that illuminated the dark road that cut through the green nature around him. The dashboard beside him suddenly lit up as his phone buzzed uncontrollably.

"Hello?"

"Hi sweetie, just wondering if you're on your way home. There's a huge thunderstorm coming our way, probably one of the last of the season." His mom's concerned voice broke through the silence form the other line.

"I know, driving through it right now. I'll be home soon."

"Okay, drive safely." A flash from behind him and Dan glanced up. Sharp headlights, set to the brightest setting, glared back at him through the small space of the mirror. The headlights grew bigger as the car drew closer. The combination of the car, the solitary confinement that it had thrown Dan into, and the growing threat of rain caused Dan's heart to skip a beat. The frantic sense that if he didn't move the car would hit him dead on became the only thought in his mind. The quiet calls as his mom called his name, when only silence responded to her could be heard as Dan numbly held the phone to his ear.

"Dan? Dan!" His quickly went from the road in front of him to the road behind him where the car only got nearer.

"Mom, I have to go. I'll be home soon." He threw his phone

into the passenger seat next to him. His hands gripped the steering wheel, and the car quickly veered to the next lane. Dan looked over his shoulder, wanting to catch the driver's face as the car quickly sped by. But the car only turned his signal on for a second, and then was suddenly right back in the same spot it was a minute ago.

The headlights seemed to blare even brighter, a harsh white that glistened against the raindrops that were littered all along the car.

"What the hell! Get off my ass!" It was the only sound besides the pitter-patter of rain, the choked voice of Dan. His foot pressed down on the accelerator and he sped up. The car only seemed to mirror his actions. Dan moved his car back to the original lane, feeling his tires momentarily lift off the ground as the rain came in heavier sheets against his car. The car moved as well, still maintaining a short distance between the two vehicles. Dan felt his fingers wring themselves against the steering wheel, trying beyond belief to think of a way to shake the car off of him.

His phone suddenly lit up again. The rain fell down with greater force. A clap of thunder broke through the silence and Dan felt his heart beat race more and more. In the epic battle between drivers, moving from one spot to the other, Dan finally saw an exit appear through the haze of rain that practically had blinded him from seeing the world correctly.

His car easily slid off the highway, following the dark road that led him towards an unknown place; but at least it was away from the other car. The whole entire time Dan realized that it was only him and the other car, an unsettling feeling that made him feel utterly alone and completely out of control. He harshly came to a stop, his eyes on the highway behind him the entire time that he attempted to brake. The other car continued on, kicking up a stream of rainwater behind it as the tires squealed underneath the moisture.

Dan probably sat at the light for minutes. No other cars appeared, and the colorful lightshow of red, yellow, and green flashed in his face without any regard to what his next action was. One hand was frozen to the steering wheel, the knuckles white and his fingers shaking. The other held his head as he tried to calm his heart down, which was beating wildly, his breathing a rhythmic beat along his heart rate. *He wasn't after you, he wasn't after you.* The voice in his head was horrible at convincing him it was the truth. The rain died down a bit, softly whispering with the wind as it began to only generate few drops on Dan's car. His fingers clawed against his face multiple times as he ran his face over and over again into the palm of his hands. He finally found the courage to turn his car, following the alternate route back to his home. He had only taken one look at the entrance to the highway in front of him before the panic set in again and he determinedly turned his car on a different path.

His blinking phone finally grabbed his attention, and he reached for the small black block that sat in the chair next to him. A missed call from Jamie was stamped on the screen. Dan felt a buzz of excitement grip him as he flipped open the phone, immediately dialing her number back.

"Hey, Jamie. Sorry I missed your call." Dan's voice was quiet, but still dribbles of thrill wanted to burst forth in a shout as he talked to the only person who seemed to keep him sane. Keeping the volume under control, he sounded reserved and composed, two feelings that he had not felt for months.

"Hey, are you on campus tonight?"

"No, I ended up going home this weekend. My mom wanted to see me."

"Oh, bummer." The sound of disappointment couldn't be hidden from her voice. Dan felt the sudden urge to turn the car around and drive back. He wanted to see Jamie, to see only her for the rest of the night. Maybe talking to her would finally give him a peaceful night of sleep. Jamie wasn't a full time treatment, and he knew that. But there was still a solidarity factor that she had, and one that Dan refused to let go.

When the world freezes for a split second, anything after that frozen moment can happen. In the brief moment when Jamie's words passed through Dan's ears, the world became frozen. And in the blink of an eye, Dan looked up. A pair of headlights stared back at him. Dan's head snapped as he did a double take. His car swerved for a split second as his hands slacked at the steering wheel. *They really are following me.*

"Dan? Dan?" The road ahead was one long, endless road. It had no other escape route, no other roads that branched off from it. Dan again felt his heart race and his hands become stiff. He sped up, but the car behind him only did the same, so that the same exact distance remained between the two cars even though the speed had altered multiple times.

"Jamie?" His voice was a hushed whisper. It might have been because he was so frightened he didn't know if he could will himself to speak. Or perhaps it came from the crazy notion that that driver could hear him. The phone conversation between Jamie and him had all the potential of being recorded, and that thought scared him more than anything. Jamie could be in danger. The killers, the cops, whoever was following Dan, could be tracking down those closest to him. Jamie, his mom, his family. *They're after me.*

"Dan? Dan, what's going on?" The car was getting closer, and Dan could finally pick out a black figure in the front seat. A man, clothed in darkness, was inching closer. An eerie feeling crept through Dan's body.

"Jamie, someone's following me."

"What do you mean? Dan—" The phone cut out and another clap of thunder entered the earth. The car behind him suddenly cranked forward, a ghastly sound emanating from its engine like the roar of a beast that wanted to gulp Dan up. He drew the phone away from his face, staring at the completely black screen.

"Jamie?" There was no answer. The car suddenly was feet away from him, and there was no other lane to move to this time. There was no other way to go. "Jamie!"

His car swerved. His phone flew from his hand and the brakes screeched underneath him. The ditch was drawing ever closer and so was a murky green and brown puddle of grass, drowning in the water that fell from the sky.

Dan's eyes were stuck on the car behind him. He turned in his seat as his car finally sunk into the soaked grass, his tires spinning up mud on either side of his car. The man in the other car looked directly at him, a blurred face and shadowed brow that just as suddenly was gone as he drove his car at a dangerous level of speed down the gray road. His breathing was labored, but his body lay slumped in the seat. His head was sinking further and further down till it lay against the cold glass window. His eyes were glued to the tiny raindrops that still landed on the window, the tiny tendrils that moved in the shape of veins against pale skin transfixing Dan. He finally reached for his phone that lay lifelessly in the back seat where he had thrown it. The phone was alive again, lighting up with life. The dull ringing was the only sound in the car.

"Mom?"

"Hello Dan, it's been a while."

"Yeah, I guess it has."

"I see you stopped coming to the individual appointments."

"Yeah, they weren't really working for me."

"You only went to one session."

"Again, wasn't working for me."

"So, you're not willing to give it another shot."

"Nope."

"Interesting, would've have pegged you as a quitter."

(Pause)

"What the hell is that supposed to mean?"

"What I see in you Dan, is a harsh exterior that wants to put up the good fight; but in reality you want to try your hardest at everything. You want to be able to say that you accomplished those goals that you had worked so hard."

"Speaking into a tape recorder about my feelings isn't a goal of mine, it's just plain stupid."

"So you rather have the sessions with me?"

(Pause)

"I'm not going to give you credit. You think you're so special, don't you Doc?"

"Why did you address me as that in the tape? You've never done that before."

"Why does it matter?"

"Well, for starters it's rude and condescending."

"Hmm, guess I don't seem to care too much anymore."

"Why not?"

"What?"

"Why don't you care anymore?"

"Haven't we jumped through this hoop already?"

"Maybe we have, but each session also carries new occurrences and new experiences that you have feelings about. So in accordance with this session, what is making you not care?"

"Because it's all trivial bullshit!"

(Pause)

"So what to you isn't trivial?"

"My family. Myself…Jamie."

"Why do you say that? Is school trivial, are the daily actions that you do every single day trivial?"

"Yes."

"Why?"

"Because it doesn't fucking matter! Who cares if I go to class on Monday? What the hell difference is it going to make?"

"Going to class is working towards the degree that you're studying, which in turn is working towards the career that you'll chose to work at for the rest of your life—"

"That's all just as trivial to me."

"Why?"

(Pause)

"They're after me.

(Pause)

"Who is?"

"The cops. The men who killed her. Both. I haven't a clue who. But they keep following me."

"What do you mean?"

"They came to my apartment; they stopped in front of my house. One guy followed me in his car as I was driving home."

"Perhaps he was taking the same route as you?"

"Oh well, gee thanks for the support! That's fucking bullshit, the guy was following me, tailing me, practically drove me off the road. And soon they'll come to the house and harass my family. And they probably know I see Jamie, so they'll go after her.

"No one is going after you're family or Jamie. The police have nothing to use against you and the murderers are mostly likely in custody—"

"I sat there watching the whole time! They clearly saw my face! Why would they not be after me? All I have to do is look like I'm going to the cops and then they'll kill me too!"

"Dan, I assure you that no one is after you. You don't even know who the girl was that was murdered."

(Pause)

"Did you know who the girl was?"

"Why the hell does that matter? They're still coming after me."

"Dan, answer the question."

"What?"

"Did you know who the girl was?"

"What the hell? No I didn't. That's not the point, listen they're after me!"

"No they are not."

"Yes they are."

"Dan, if they were after you they would have killed you already. And they have no reason to come to your family or Jamie. This would be a very elaborate plot if they did kill everyone that you're in contact with."

"Why do you not suspect that? Why is that not an option for you?"

"Because it is highly unlikely. This happened months ago Dan."

"Who the hell cares what the time frame of this all was? They're after me."

"NO, they're not."

"We have to find a way to protect my family. And I need to tell Jamie—"

"Dan, there is no reason to do any such thing."

"You're supposed to help me, why aren't you helping me?"

"Because you're not in danger, Dan."

"So what it's all in my head? A guy, in his car, drove me off the side of the road. He sped his car up till the point that he was going to hit me. And on campus, people are watching me all the time."

"People are allowed to look at you on campus Dan. And as I said before, the man was probably taking a very similar route."

"Stop saying that!"

"You have no connection to the girl; you don't even know her…"

"Stop saying I didn't know her. I don't care about the fact that I didn't know her. The point is I still saw it and now I'm in trouble and you don't believe me."

"That's because you're in very safe hands and if something hasn't happened in months I doubt anything will."

"Just believe me. The guy was following me!"

"Dan, calm down."

"I don't want to fucking calm down. They're after me!"

"They're not after you!"

"Fuck you!"

(Door slam)

(Sigh)

"November 12th. Dan Braddock clearly showing signs of paranoia, insomnia, lack of eating. Keep careful watch."

# X

A roadside never bears any form of importance until it becomes the only thing within one's sight that is completely outside of one's grasp. Set in a monastic gray background, the black road shimmers with the occasional white stripe. The white stripes in the middle of the road are there ideally for the common eye to keep straight forward; an insignia that keeps people going down the correct path. Perhaps then, it was ideal that the white strips meant absolutely nothing to Dan as he had swerved off the road.

The roadside, whereby it is attained by curving off the road rather than taking the allotted straight path, became the only certain thing to Dan. At the moment, stuck in his mud splattered and soaked car, the gentle dip into the woods that roadside yielded was welcoming to Dan. He found the broken seam in the effortlessly flat land around him, the tiny dip that signaled the beginning of the roadside, to be the perfect spot to sit. Here, no one could necessarily see him. Drivers would be moving so fast that they would have to continue on their way, and eventually would have to forget about the young man who was sitting shocked and unmoving in his vehicle. They would continue to follow that commanding straight road that lay ahead of them.

Dan had moved past the moments of starring with blurred vision at the steering wheel. His hands eventually unhooked themselves, pain shooting through the tiny muscles in each finger as it uncurled in a sickly fashion. His hands were now resting at his side, and his body had sagged towards the window. The cold glass rested against his perspiring forehead, cooling down the insatiable rising temperature that had grown within him. The moment in between his body being bent close and seized and suddenly melted in relaxation was an incredible incident. Dan could feel, beginning in his feet, the gentle wave of calm wash over him. His body that was rigid with anxiety suddenly molded to the old material of the car seat. And it was in this dissolved position that he sat in for minutes, staring out into the roadside.

The headlights of his dad's car danced against the droplets of rain that still sprinkled all over Dan's car, as if mocking him for the mistake that he made. A tow truck appeared in the distance just as Dan silently watched his father's car slowly power down; his body instinctively sinking lower into the car seat in order to hide from his father's derision. The man that lumbered out of the car was slightly bigger than his son, holding a built figure that at first could startle a person. It was without question that Dan's father worked daily on his physique, but the carefree nature in which he held himself proved the world that he could be one of the gentlest beings around. In this instant though, Dan could see the look in his father's eye as he walked closer to the car. Disappointment and utter frustration were inked in his father's face, an undeniable confrontation brewing up between the two looks that father and son gave. Dan dutifully rolled down the window, his fingers brushing against the cool metal of the car door. His father planted himself directly in front of the window, beads of rainwater sticking to every pore of his face.

"You're going to leave me standing here in the rain all night? I already drove this far to pick up your butt."

And so it began. One simple sentence brought back every notion of tension that Dan had thought would have disappeared after he spent almost three years not living underneath his father's roof. It's not that he and his father wanted conflict between them, but as Dan grew older, a greater sense that the two men of the family would grow up to live very different lifestyles had become apparent.

For Dan, it was nothing that necessarily should yield a cold relationship. For his father, it was a hard challenge to show pride in his son's actions when he clearly disapproved of them. At this very moment, a father stared severely at his son. And his son, normally readily equipped with the same harshness, had all but given in and given up. He didn't want to fight tonight.

They climbed into his father's car with a palpable silence. However, in this case of fatherhood, silence was always his father's way of saying to Dan that everything would be okay. Rather ignore it and brush it under the rug than make it a bigger dilemma than it already was. Strictly speaking, both men wanted nothing more to do than drive back to the house with no conversation, sleep for a night, and forget the whole thing ever happened. Though it would be impossible to forget about the mud splattered and smashed car, the tow truck that was now following them, and the stack of money that would be whisked away from the bank in order to pay for the damages that Dan created all on his own accord.

Without protest, Dan maneuvered himself so that he was facing the passenger window. He curiously watched the tow truck behind him, waiting to see another car suddenly emerge behind the second vehicle, creating a caravan of people that all seemed to be following him against his will.

"Mom's worried about you." Dan paused before glancing over at his father. The man's eyes were plastered to the road ahead of him, his jaw clenched firmly as if this were the most embarrassing conversation that he could be having with his son. A slight smile came to Dan's face as he heard the actually translation amongst the spoken words.

*What the hell were you thinking?!*

"Well I'm fine." The remark came out more curtly than Dan wanted, an immediate grimace appearing on his face as he saw his dad seethe with growing frustration.

"Really, Dan?"

"Yes I —"

"Cause you just ran your car into the side of the road! So unless you have a better explanation that just being dumb, I'd like it hear it." Dan looked over at his father, his eyes wide. Never had it seemed that his father could be as angry as he was now. The fights that had occurred in the past were snide, cynical comments that were thrown back at each other. But now, his father was throwing Dan full-blown anger that couldn't be tamed. The desire to spill every thought that was going through his mind at the time that he felt it best to drive his car off the side of the road was overbearing.

Instead, his jaw tightened and his teeth clamped up, grinding back and forth against each other like two rocks as he tried to force the unbearable feeling down. In the silence he watched his father take deep breaths, his eyes turning in every direction but directly at Dan. His son was the last person he wanted to see at the moment, but the situation was too great to pay no heed to.

"You should still talk to your mom when we get home," there was a feeble attempt to reconcile the scene that had just transpired. The heavy noise of Dan's teeth was the only remark that he made to his father. In confused glances, his father's eyes suddenly went from the road to his son. The shadows that lay themselves all over his son's face revealed a deeper conflict than he had ever seen in his son. Dan's face looked positively tormented, an anguish of feelings that all wanted to reveal themselves at the same moment.

"Are you…are you grinding your teeth?" Dan's breath caught. He fumbled a cough, placing his hand over his mouth, which ached a dull pain that he had become too familiar with. Without answering the question, he leaned against the window.

His father sighed in defeat. Another fight was over, and he felt like he had lost another battle in order to break the walls of the fortress that his son had constructed around himself. Dan remained still, feigning sleep as he stared out at the passing roadside. The incoherent pattern of the grass, the tiny bubbles of earth that peaked over the black asphalt were all that Dan watched. The misprints in the perfect set land around him, the uneven ground and leaked imperfections of the roadside were comforts, as they seemed to mimic every disjointed moment that was in Dan's life.

As a mother, she had always told herself that she would have to find a way to not worry so much. But Dan's voice when he called quelled everything about that goal that his mother had set for herself. When the phone rang and his voice was on the other line it sounded so small. And that was the only way his mother knew how to describe it.

There was no assurance that he could give her when he called. There was nothing in his voice at all. It was a fainting echo of the voice that used to inhabit her son's. She knew that his mind was completely there, that a wandering thought was taking half of his conscious mind all the time to a place that he couldn't escape from. The sense of this had started weeks ago when Dan had visited the house last, but now it was pronounced, more visible. And suddenly, she felt too distanced as his mother to do anything to resolve it.

The television was humming quietly in the background of her mind when she heard the garage door creak open. The two men lumbered in. Her husband looked tired and worn, but still held himself with a sense of assertiveness. He didn't want to worry her. He laid the keys on the kitchen counter, glancing up at the staircase to his left.

"I'll take the car in the morning to get fixed, shouldn't cost too much."

"That sounds good," her voice was meek, a fading whisper as she watched Dan stroll into the kitchen. His body was bent over with fatigue, his eyes planted firmly on the window that yielded only the dark of the night. His eyes were weary, but yet still open wide with fretfulness.

"Dan…" even saying his name seemed like a futile attempt to try and pry the answer out of him.

"I'm fine Mom. I'm just really stressed out at school; I guess I wasn't pay attention to where I was going for a split second." His voice was dripping in deceit that he was hoping to pass directly over his mom without her noticing. It was a failed shot.

"Dan, if there's something you want to talk about—"

"I'm fine, really. I'm just tired. I think I'm just going to go to bed."

His mother wanted nothing more than to talk to Dan, but he refused to open up anymore as he climbed slowly up the staircase, his shoulders still slumped over. Like a ghost, he silently walked into his room, dropping his things carelessly on the ground before collapsing into his bed. His phone lit up next to him, but he ignored it, shutting the device off before closing his eyes in effort to drown out every sound around him. But yet, as he faded into a restless sleep, he still felt he heard the whisper of his name in the shadows.

"Jamie?"

"Dan! Holy cow, you're alive. What happened the other night? Are you okay?"

"Yeah, I'm fine. I guess I was just really tired when I was driving the other night."

(Pause)

"You said someone was following you."

(Pause)

"Dan, is everything okay?"

"There was someone Jamie, I swear."

"I believe you, Dan—"

"There was a guy in a car, following me the whole time!"

"Dan, I already said I believe you!"

(Pause)

"I'm sorry; I just…my therapist doesn't believe me."

"I didn't know you were seeing a therapist."

"Would you be surprised if I said there's not a lot you know about me?"

"Not at all."

(Pause)

"You're coming back to campus soon, right?"

"Did I tell you he wants to put me on meds?"

"What? Your therapist? No, you didn't say anything about that."

"Yeah, he does. He says that it will help calm me down or something. What the hell do I need meds for?"

"I don't think you do. I mean someone following you is a serious thing. He should be paying attention to that. Of course someone is going to be upset if someone is watching them, that doesn't mean medicine to calm you down is going to fix it."

(Pause)

"Just don't take them, you know?"

"Yeah…I guess…"

"So, you'll be back soon?"

"Yeah, I'll be back soon."

(Pause)

"Good."

"I want to prescribe you some medication."

(Pause)

"What the hell?"

"It's for your panic attacks; it'll help calm you down."

"I'm not having panic attacks."

"Dan, the last few sessions you've shown symptoms and told me incidences in which—"

"What, are you spying on me?"

"That is a ridiculous accusation, Dan. But this behavior, coming from you right this instant is why I want to give you some medication."

"I don't need medication; there is nothing wrong with me."

"Now you say that."

"What?"

"How many times do you sit up at night wondering why you act the way you do? Wondering why you can't just be normal?"

"Seeing someone being killed is a pretty damn good reason to not be…no, I don't have to answer those questions!"

"Admit it Dan, because we both know that the thought occurs to you frequently."

"You know, you're not a quintessential doctor."

"I've never written down on my resume that I would be."

"There is nothing wrong with me."

"Are you saying that to convince me or yourself?"

"Shut the fuck up!"

"Dan, I'm not drugging you, I'm not saying that you should be locked away and given electric shock. I understand your situation—"

"Are you trying to convince me of that?"

(Sigh)

"How impatient are you with me?"

"Dan, that is definitely not the point right now."

"How difficult is it working with me?"

"Dan—"

"How many times have you just wanted to say, "fuck it" and not speak to me anymore?"

"That's never going to happen, Dan, I'm here to help you."

"By pumping me full of drugs?"

(Pause)

"Dan, hear me out. With your situation and the past numerous experiences that you've had, I think it'd be wise that you take some medication. It'll help calm you down, help you focus on school—"

"I don't want to focus on school."

"Well, it can at least get you to the end of the semester."

(Pause)

"Have you told your parents you want to take a break from school?"

"No."

"Who have you told?"

"Jamie, that's it."

"What does she think?"

"I dunno…she doesn't really understand why I want to take a break from school."

"What excuse are you giving her? I'm assuming you still haven't told her."

"No, I haven't."

"Maybe, if she's someone that you know you can trust she would be a good person to confide in before talking to your parents."

(Pause)

"Would the medicine really help?"

"Yes, it's only a pill, nothing major. But I think that it could help, at least ease your mind if nothing else."

(Pause)

"Why don't you believe me?"

"Excuse me?"

"Jamie believes me."

"Dan, I—"

"I don't think I'm going to come to a session for a while."

"Dan, I don't think—"

"How about this? I don't care what you think! I'm tired of all this, I need a break. You want me to focus on class, great, then let me do just that and let me be for a bit!"

"Is this what Jamie told you to do?"

"This has nothing to do with her! This is my decision!"

"I don't think this is the right decision for you to be making right now."

(Chair moves)

"Guess who still doesn't give a shit?"

(Door slams)

# XI

Dan could have yelled at the room to stop spinning, but there was no point. The room would jokingly rebuke him, and continue on its relentless whirling with Dan as its axis. The phone sitting on the nightstand buzzed, inching closer and closer to Dan across the polished wood, yet his fingers didn't even itch to be closer to the object. He stared up at the ceiling fan that moved at a perfectly set rhythm and didn't falter in its course. His fingers brushed the soft bed sheets to the coarse paper of the book that lay abandoned at his side. But Dan still remained indifferent to everything. It was day nine of the medications.

Hours held no concern to Dan anymore. In fact, he had begun to realize that time was a luxury that people squandered abhorrently. And he was bought in by the idea of watching the slippery demon of time glide through his fingers, yet felt no regard to its consequence. And the consequence was drawing closer and would soon face him head on. In spite of that Dan knew that he'd be able to stare right at it with the same lack of enthusiasm that he did the ceiling fan.

The perfect numbness that had settled into his bones both confused and elated Dan. At first, when he fully felt the effects of the drugs that he had been given, it was like a downward spiral that could shed no light and bear no sign of release. He sat in his room, feeling no guilt for not moving, for not eating or drinking. He moved his fingers slowly over various things, a book that lay tucked underneath his bed, to the remote that controlled his television set. And the sudden feeling came over him that it didn't matter what he did that day. He could finish the novel that had been feebly trying to inch its way out from underneath his bed, or he could watch mindless hours of television. Neither mattered to him. And in that aspect neither did anything that could possibly occur that day.

The first day of this realization gave way to the second day of him trying it again, but this time with an assurance that he would create an effort and motivation to accomplish something. But yet again, he roamed through his room, through his apartment, even to the library to glance frequently at his books. But none of it mattered to him. The trail of the third day was an experience that he never wanted to place on his body again: it was the attempt to not take the medication that had been prescribed to him.

The pain that exploded through his body, like a giant rake that was able to pinpoint every nerve in his brain and every muscle in his arms and legs and scrap relentlessly against them, was a pain that crippled him into reaching for the jar of pills and swoop a handful into his mouth without count. The haze that covered his mind within minutes was an incredible sensation of exhilaration as his heart slowed to a steady beat and confusion as he began to fall in and out of recollection.

Sometime within that day Jamie had come into his room. His glazed eyes were moving slowly back and forth between her and the bright colors of the television. Her eyes, which normally were supportive and consoling, were daggers. She sat firmly at the edge of the bed, staring at him with the knuckles of her fingers turning white as she gripped the blanket tightly underneath her hand.

"You shouldn't be taking those," she stated curtly. Dan looked at her closely, at the way her lips pursed up in disgust, her eyes lingering at the medicine bottle for a brief instant and igniting new anger.

"They make me feel better." Those were the only words that Dan felt himself able to speak. Jamie instantly stood, reaching for the doorknob with an absurd sense of purpose; purpose that for a fleeting instant Dan was jealous of.

"This isn't you, Dan." She left, slamming the door, and Dan fell into an obscene slumber that left him unapproachable and unmoving for hours of the day.

The state in which he walked the earth with no regard was how he entered the week of finals. Instead of being held down by the heavy weight of determination that everyone else had, he briskly walked from final to final with a sense of elation that it'd all be behind him in three days' time. The jealousy that people have to him, seeing a fellow student walk into a final with all the confidence in the world, only gave him a greater will power to move listlessly from one test to another.

Only one person saw the medicine-induced illusion that Dan had fixed on himself: Jamie. Her eyes that at one time had uplifted Dan, now only held a disappointment that made Dan resent her whenever she appeared in front of him. Something between them was ruined, and all that was left was a strained acquaintance that Dan wanted to build back up, but found he was unable to put forth the effort. Likewise, Jamie still would stand by his side, walking with him to every location that he wished as if it were her duty. But the light of liveliness that had been in her eyes, the faint color of joy whenever she would talk with Dan had faded. In its wake was a wave of annoyance touched with a faint sprinkle of regret. Unlike Dan's resentment, Jamie held a little bit of hope, yet Dan was gleefully watching it dwindle away without bearing in mind the greater loss he would receive.

Even now, as he walked with her from his last final, Dan could sense a pressure pushing Jamie away from him. She had used to be a continual support, a presence that was always trying to lift his spirits back up. With Jamie, he was able to briefly forget about the constant nightmare that haunted him. But now, Jamie was the person who fought against him the most, constantly contradicting him and arguing for the mere sake of making him relive that harsh memory.

Their steps were quick, as if Dan were trying to outrun her

back to the apartment in order to leave her utterly behind. Jamie took quick, numbly steps next to him, not missing a beat, nor missing the growing anger that was welling up in Dan's eyes. His head had begun to throb, he suddenly became astonishingly aware that he had just taken all of his finals, and he couldn't for the life of him even remember if he had taken a second to prepare for any of them.

A wave of worry washed throughout his entire body, and suddenly a gush of exhaustion took over. His eyes hurt from the bright light of the sun, and Jamie without turning her head to see what direction she was walking, had a small smirk planted on her lips. Dan hefted his backpack, taking a deep breath as a needle of pain suddenly stuck itself in the front of his forehead. His fingers grasped to his skin where sweat had begun to gather and pool. All the while Jamie walked next to him, only as a silent observer.

"What?" Dan asked sharply, feeling her eyes roaming all over with an acidulous smile that made him want to smack her across the face.

"I told you not to take the drugs."

"Excuse me but when did you become a doctor?" The sarcasm swarmed out of Dan's mouth like a cloud of locust plaguing the area in which they stood. Jamie stopped, grabbing his sweatshirt and whirling Dan back around. His footsteps became uneasy, his knees crumbling weakly underneath him. By the time he caught himself, he suddenly became increasingly more aware that people had begun to look over. Unable to meet anyone's gaze, his eyes firmly met Jamie's, which were ignited with the same passion.

"At least I don't hide anything from you." And there it was, plain and simple. She had obtained the power to break Dan down and slowly build him back up, all with the intent of finding out what he wished to shelter most from anyone hearing. She was in complete control of everything, up to what Dan would say next and how she would be able to finally confess what he was trying to hide. "I know you're hiding something Dan."

*Oh god, she knows! How the hell does she know?* A sudden wave of paranoia swept over Dan as the last of the medications that he took last night finally began to wear off. The world suddenly became claustrophobic. He was a player on a stage and everyone in the audience had turned to face him, and only him. Jamie stood front and center with the accusing look, while people around her turned slowly, their eyes meeting his. Some laughed, other scorned and every once in a while there would be the few amongst the crowed that held the same look as Jamie. The *"I know what you saw"* look; the incriminating look that had been driving Dan insane and filling him with hours of thoughts that tortured and meddled with every sane thought that he had ever had.

To watch the world move in slow motion, as pairs of eyes suddenly remained fixated on Dan, was a scene that one only pictures in films. One can imagine it happening, but it never really escapes into reality, it remains only an imagined dream. But Dan was watching with growing unease as he felt hundreds of eyes bear down on him. Dan's eyes scattered from the boy looking at him with headphones on, to the girl who had momentarily stopped talking as she took a mean stare at him, as if he had interrupted the most important conversation of her life. His eyes then trailed to the two men, both dressed in suits that had walked out of the nearest academic building. One held a cell phone, the other a cigarette. But as if in sync, their faces were lifted to find the solitary boy who was not stuck in the slow motion stance that the world had taken on, but rather was ticking like a time bomb as his heart began to race faster and faster. *They know me; they're walking straight towards me. Run Dan!* But his feet didn't move. And Jamie still held onto his arm, and her fingers were gripping like a trap, wrapped tightly around him.

*Let me go! Get away from me!*

"Tell me what's going on Dan, you can trust me!" *No I can't, I can't trust anyone in this world.* His mind stared at the bottle of pills that lay next to his bedside, the pills that had blurred his mind for days now, brainwashing him into a civilized world that didn't exist, and snapping reality away from his thoughts. *Is Doc in on it, too?*

"Dan!" Her eyes were wide, and they held a fear that Dan reciprocated. "Dan," she whispered softly. "Talk to me." But Dan felt himself step back, his feet dragging across the hard pavement.

"Get away from me," the whisper that barely escaped his lips was almost inaudible, Jamie taking a step closer to hear him. Her fingers grazed along his cold hand. Sweat dripped down his face. The two men stepped closer. The smoke that flitting out of the man's cigarette swirled in the air. The smoke wouldn't go back in; no matter how much Dan willed it, the smoke still swirled in the air, a slow dance up to the heavens. It wouldn't return, the man would never taste that same amount of smoke. And no matter how much Dan willed it, the scene in the alley did happen. And he could no longer run from it. He looked back over to Jamie, who stood in front of him with a hand still begging to be held in front of her. A red glow had turned over onto her face, catching against every pore and enveloping her. Dan's heart stopped and he shuttered for breath.

"Stay away from me!" The shout echoed against every wall that it bounced against. Within seconds it had made it back to Dan's ears. The man with the cigarette paused, the stick of nicotine inches from his face, glowing a dull orange as it began to burn out. Likewise, the man next to him suddenly stopped from pulling the cell phone from his ear, and then just as quickly began frantically dialing once more. Dan sucked in a breath, his lungs contracting painfully.

A tear clutched to Jamie's cheek, her face looked defeated. People stopped and stared and the judgment that Dan felt was too much to bear. He took a step back. His body crumbled to the ground as his legs gave out, the stone that he tripped on bouncing from underneath the momentum of his foot. On the ground, Dan shamefully looked up. Jamie still stood there, her face cloaked in crimson.

"Stay away!" He scrambled back to his feet. Whispers floated through the air, as people looked from were Jamie stood to Dan, their eyes wide with astonishment. His body felt like lead, but he still was able to force himself away, running far from the scene.

The earth around him shattered, nothing was the same and nothing could be changed. He couldn't go back.

"Hello?"

"What the hell did you give me?"

(Pause)

"Dan?"

"No shit it's Dan, who else would it be?"

"How did you get my cell phone number?"

"Answer my question first!"

"What do you mean what did I give you? What have you been doing with your medications?"

"Don't turn the tables on me as if this is my fault! I took that prescription and suddenly I didn't care about anything in the world. I could have been run over by a car and I wouldn't have cared! Are you with them?"

"With who Dan?"

"The people who are after me!"

"No one is after you—"

"Cut the shit and tell me the fucking truth!"

"This is the truth Dan! I'm not coming after you!"

"Why are you brainwashing me with the meds then, huh? I'm not taking them anymore!"

"I'm trying to help you Dan, whether or not you want to accept the help is entirely up to you."

(Pause)

"They're going to find me."

"What happened Dan?"

"Jamie's with them."

"Dan, what happened?"

"I was just walking with her, and suddenly she asked about what I saw and then…then everyone was watching. It was like they all knew…"

"Dan?"

(Silence)

"Dan?"

"They'll go for my family…"

"Dan! Listen to me. I'm here to help you! I need you to listen to me. There is no one after you and no one is going to come for your family. Dan, where are you right now?"

(Silence)

"Dan? Dan!"

"I have to make it stop. I have to stop them from going after my family."

"Dan, where are you?"

(Silence)

"Dan?"

(Phone hangs up)

"Shit!"

"Mrs. Braddock?"

"Yes?"

"Hello, this is Doctor Alan Fuller. I'm calling in regards to Dan. Is he home?"

"No, he's at school. May I ask why you're calling?"

(Pause)

"Dr. Fuller?"

"I need you to go pick up your son right away."

"What? Why? What's wrong with Dan?"

"I believe that something serious is wrong with Dan."

"What? What is going on with my son? What you do you mean something serious is wrong with him?"

"Please Mrs. Braddock—"

"No, you tell me right now what is wrong with my son and why I have to get him? Did he call you?"

"Yes he did. He was very upset and not in the right mind."

"Not in the right mind? What medication did you give him?"

"It's not the medication. Please understand that Dan will be fine. He just needs to come home right away. Please call me immediately when he gets home. I need to see him right away. I'm sorry though, I have to go."

"Dr. Fuller?"

(Silence)

"Dr. Fuller?!"

# XII

Dan heard the screeching tires as his parents finally pulled up to the apartment. His heart had not stopped racing, and the world still pointed an accusatory finger directly at him. Every person that he had passed on his way back to the apartment seemed to be staring right at him. Their eyes were unmoving, only lingering as he frantically ran past. His call to Dr. Fuller did nothing to ease his worry, but only confirmed and increased his suspicions that this whole time the man was out to harm him. And Jamie…his mind kept going back to her face. Her eyes had softened with worry and he suddenly remembered the first time he had seen her, when her face was washed red with blood. He tried to block the image from his mind, but it kept still in his mind's eye, hovering like a deep seeded secret that was ready to burst forth with tremendous force. Every time he shut his eyes it was always the same.

His parents stepped out of the car, the slam of the car door from his father and the hurried footsteps of his mother's heels echoing across the buildings that were lined along the street. His mother's shouts were heard above the sounds of traffic, a fervent call that was impossible to ignore.

Dan stepped forth from the doorway and was immediately swept into the open arms of his mother. She mumbled words over and over, assuring herself that he was safe and well. These were the two feelings that Dan knew he was a million miles away from and would be unable to obtain again. The steps to the car seemed to take forever; each footstep lingering too much of the movement between lifting off the ground, sweeping forward in the air, and coming back in contact with the ground below. Each movement made Dan's body groan in pain; shaking as strength was ebbed away with every movement. He silently slipped into the car, throwing his belongings next to him and sprawled across the bag that held weeks of dirty clothes. The car sped away, his parents glancing at him every once in a while in the rearview mirror, till finally Dan felt the glances too many times, and turned his back to the time.

His eyes picked out every fiber of the fabric of the car seat directly in front of them, his nose brushing against the worn patterned seat. Each criss-cross was perfectly met and fashioned so that one stitch wasn't out of place. Each had its own place, and was matching in every way to the stitch next to it and the one that followed after in the infinite amount of rows that were facing Dan. His eyes drooped every so often, and then suddenly the car would turn red, dripping with the disgusting color. His eyes would spring back open. But eventually, the continuous pattern of the stitches soon became obsolete and boring. Dan felt his eyes close once more, and though the red was still there, like a beating heart inside of his head, the image had finally vanished. All he saw was the color, the least favorite in Dan's world.

They all entered the house without a word. His father brought in the bags of things that Dan had packed for home; his mother softly placed her purse on the kitchen counter. Dan glanced around at every object as it were the first and last time he had ever seen them. It all seemed so ordinary, and yet so benign. It all meant nothing. His father gave Dan a hard glance, but placed a soft reassuring pat to Dan's back as he lumbered into the living room. His mother lingered in the kitchen, facing her son. His eyes seemed lost, as if this world around him were a foreign land.

"Your sister is at a friend's. She'll be back later tonight." Dan nodded without so much as glancing at his mother. "Dan…"

"I don't want to talk about it."

"Dan—"

"No!"

His dad had stood back up and had walked back into the doorway of the kitchen. His eyes were laden with fury; as if Dan was threatening his mother and his father would have to be the one to intervene.

"Dr. Fuller called," his father stated, a booming voice that shattered the uncomfortable silence that had covered the room. Dan spun around, his breath catching in his throat.

"He what?"

"Said you were in trouble. Demanded that we pick you up right away." The sudden dread that flowed through Dan promoted the images of his family dying before his eyes, just as she had died before his eyes. "You better tell us why he was saying that."

"It's not safe..." Dan whispered. His dad, arms crossed, stepped closer, bearing down on his son.

"What?"

Dan glanced between both of his parents, his eyes wide with fear. His mother trembled like a child being scolding for misbehaving.

"Dan," she said gently. "What is going on?"

It is said that a child can always trust a parent. That the love they bear for their children is the greatest love ever, because it has no limits. A parent cannot hate you, cannot be disappoint in a child. They only bear an undying love that cannot be met by anyone else. But this was exactly what hindered Dan from reliving his deepest secret. It was their trust that was on the line, for once they knew, they were in the same danger that he was in. Once he told them, their love for their son would change. Morally, he was obligated to help her, yet he only watched her die. Morally, how could a parent love a son who witnessed a murder, and did nothing to stop it?

Dan sidestepped, unable to provide any sort of answer to his parents' questions. And in the silence that he provided to the conversation, it only prompted an unceasing flow of further questions from the mouth of his parents.

"Did you do something?"

"Why did Dr. Fuller give you medication?"

"What is the medication doing?"

"Dan, tell us what is going on? What happened?"

It all became too much.

"Enough!" he yelled. His parents froze. They were unable to move closer to their son, to provide a comforting touch. Yet they were also too startled and worried to move away. His mother finally looked up at him, finding the courage to meet her son's eyes. Tears rolled down her cheeks.

"What's wrong with you Dan?" she sobbed. It was the heartbreaking, gut-wrenching sound of her crying that made Dan's blood flow faster, his heart beat at a quicker speed, his mind to race with images of every way that the same people who had killed her would kill his family; all just to get back to Dan; to leer in his face and laugh with a condescending victory of Dan's ultimate silence over what he had experienced.

"I…I can't stay here." He took a step back. His father hastily moved out of his way, as if Dan were a diseased stranger that had tried to grab him and infect him. His father's eyes stared at Dan as if he couldn't recognize his son anymore. His mother only held her face within her hands, sobs emanating from beneath her clenched fingertips.

"It's not safe."


He had locked himself in his room, unable to move from his bed once he sat down on it. He could hear their voices, their arguments growing in fierceness as they began to blame each other for the way that Dan had turned out. They turned the tables on themselves at first, blaming their own parenting skills for the lack of a successful son that they had created. Then they turned on each other, blaming the other for being too needy, for not being there to help support Dan.

He listened with every fiber in his being, his fingers clenching and twisting the sheet that lay beneath him. The conversation down stairs continued for hours, until the squeak of a door signaled that his sister had returned home. The hush that came from downstairs was a feeble attempt to show his sister that nothing was wrong. A knock came when her dainty footsteps finally made it up the stairs, but Dan instead ignored her; though it ached to hear her walk away from him.

The sun slowly blinked goodnight as the earth faded into darkness, yet Dan had not moved from the spot on his bed. He heard his parents still discussing downstairs, but at quiet whispers that neither his sister nor he could discern from upstairs. And finally, he heard the lights shut off, and his parents slowly take each step up the stairs. He felt the presence of his father pausing in front of his door, and then without a word retreat into his own bedroom. The house remained silent. Dan stared at the blank wall of his bedroom, his fingers still wringing the now wrinkled sheet. His mind was going in every direction, through all of the possibilities. And he knew that there was only so much he could do to protect them, and so much that he would have to sacrifice in doing so.

He didn't exactly know what prompted him to walk downstairs, yet without a sound he crept downstairs. The moonlight lit up the road through the giant window in his living room. The white glow was so bright that shadows could be seen of the trees, the mailboxes and the small animals that flitted about in the night. And within the dark path of his driveway, Dan strained to look, but finally focused on the figure that stood there. It was the figure of Jamie. He didn't question her presence, only opened his door, and walked out.

She stood with her arms clutched to her sides, her hair flowing down either side of her face. When Dan stepped closer, he noticed tears reflecting off the moonlight that lit up her face.

"Jamie?" She sniffed, wiping her face with her hand before tucking it back into the pocket of her sweatshirt.

"I'm sorry." Dan stepped closer, almost wishing that he would blink and she'd be gone.

"What are you doing here?"

"I came to apologize. I shouldn't have pried. I'm so sorry." Her last words faded into her choked sobs. Dan felt his hand reach out for her, but stop within inches of her face.

"Jamie?" his voice brought her face up to his, and her eyes, though blurred with tears, stared directly at him. "I don't know what to do. I don't even know what's real anymore." The despair that clutched in his throat was a brick wall that suddenly smacked him across the face. He had become utterly lost and held the belief that there was nothing that could bring him back from the dark hole that he had dug for himself. His fingers drew closer and then were tracing themselves along Jamie's cheek. She took a step closer to him, and he relished in the warmth that she brought with her. His fingers still remained on her cheek as he bent his head down, his lips softly brushing along hers.

"What was that for?" she whispered when they finally looked at each other again. Dan tried to utter words, but for a moment he was at a loss and had no idea what made him kiss her.

"I just…I needed to make sure this was happening. All of this." They stood in silence amongst the subdued night, a serene calm settling over them.

"You have to promise me something," Dan finally spoke into the darkness. Jamie seemed to be faded from his sight, a blur of an image though he tried to refocus on her face. But the night was too dark, and clouds hid the moon.

"What?"

"Promise me that you won't try to find me." He could feel her eyes widen in disbelief, unwilling to answer to his request.

"Dan—"

"Promise me." She took in a breath, tears welling in her eyes and drilling down her cheeks.

"Alright, I promise."

He closed the door with an effortless click and turned into

the living room, tracing his fingers along every single object that came along his path. His padded feet sunk into the carpeted stairs as he ascended them one by one, taking a pause between each step to encourage him that this was what he needed to do. He stopped at the top, the hallway that yielded each door to the bedrooms of the house suddenly looking much longer that it actually was, as if it were a torturous trek that Dan had to journey in order to finally reach his destination. His feet wadded along the soft carpet, coming to the door of his sister's bedroom. His fingers brushed the golden doorknob, and his breath caught in his throat.

He felt his eyes grow hot as tears obstructed his vision. Throwing his knuckles into his eyes, he wiped the tears away, and slowly opened the door. A single creak resounded off the walls, but his sister didn't move from her slumber. Dan took heavy steps to her bed, kneeling down at the end of it. He gazed at his sister, mopping up more tears as he watched her sleep. He swept his eyes along the room, to the bookshelf completely accompanied by books, to the dresser that held an assortment of discarded clothes. His eyes landed finally on her desk, where in the corner of the mirror that was over the desk did he spy a picture. It was taken the day Dan left for college. They both faced the camera, and he had his arms around her, lifting her off the ground as they both smiled and laughed.

Dan stared at the image, thinking of how much the picture was a lie. Though that moment was a happy one, minutes later his sister was crying at the prospect of her brother leaving for college, and the cheerful air that was captured in the photo was taken over by a more somber experience. Nevertheless, Dan always found that the picture made him smile. He looked back down at his sister, who still hadn't moved from the position she was sleeping in. He was a ghost that couldn't disturb her.

"I…" he hesitated. What could he possibly say that would mean anything, leave any significance, when he knew that the minute he walked from this door, everything would crumble down like tiny grains of sand as a child's fingers brush along the top of the sand castle. Unable to stand another second, he got up; his footsteps leaving indented marks on the carpet, leaving the only trace that he had ever entered the room.

The hallway, in the faint light that he had been given by the world around it, suddenly looked long. The last door at the end seemed miles away, and every step that Dan took only felt like an inch of ground covered between him and the room he aimed for. His fingers were reluctant to grab the doorknob in front of him, as if polarized to the sides of his body.

The room was flawless. Every detail of it had been measured, decorated and set perfectly as if in a photograph. There were the patterned pillows that sat idly in the armchair, plump and jovial. Each nightstand held various objects that represented the person who slept next to them. The abandoned novel with the bookmark that had barely traversed through ten pages, the cover still perfectly flat, the pages not yet worn. There was the cell phone that blinked with a quiet breath every few seconds, next to the fragile pair of reading glasses. The remote to the television across the room dangled at the edge of the nightstand, like a wavering car over a cliff. Everything was placed in the spot it should be, without thought of decisive manner, it just was.

So how did such a broken scene like this have the unlikely existence of actually occurring? Dan wondered how such an improbable event, the drastic scenario in which everything one had worked to accomplish in life suddenly wasn't all it was cracked up to be, nor what one thought it would be, could happen to his parents. They had wished for nothing more than a carefree lifestyle. *So why do I have to punish them?* Dan wondered all of this as he stood immobile in the doorway, a force stopping him from completely entering the room. His father was lying on his back, breathing softly without restraint, but his mother was on her side, facing Dan. Her forehead was creased against her hand that cradled her cheek. Every so often, her eyes would squeeze together and her head would twitch, as if she were trying to guard herself from whatever she was seeing. For a brief second, her face looked pained. Dan could feel the lulling pull from his room, the conscience that begged him to go back to his bed, lie down, and forget this ever happened. But Dan couldn't do that. He gripped the handle to the door, and clicked it shut.

"I'm sorry," Dan choked to the wooden door. It had nothing to say back.

"Hello?"

"Dr. Fuller?"

"Yes, this is he."

"Where's Dan?"

(Pause)

"I...I'm sorry what?"

"Dan's gone! Where is he?"

"Mrs. Braddock?"

"Your perceptive skills are impeccable!"

"Now I see where Dan gets his wit from."

"Don't fuck with me! Where is my son?"

"Mrs. Braddock, I have no idea where your son is. Have you tried calling the police?"

"Of course I have. He drove off though, our car is gone."

"Mrs. Braddock, he probably went for a drive—"

"You tell me whether or not my son driving alone in the middle of the night is a good idea."

(Pause)

"I'll contact the police Mrs. Braddock, inform them of the situation. Mrs. Braddock, did he say anything to you last night after you took him home."

"Nothing. He was so quiet he barely said a word. What is going on? What has he been saying to you?"

"Mrs. Braddock I'm afraid—"

"I don't care about the patient/doctor confidentially code. You've been treating my son; you put him on the medications. For months I've watched Dan become more and more closed in, completely stripping himself from everything around him. Something is going on and you need to tell me right now what is happening to my son!"

"Mrs. Braddock, I will do everything to help insure the safety and health of your son. But right now this is a matter that you should consult with the police. They will do a much better job of finding your son than I will."

"But you know what he's thinking. You know what's going on in his head. If anyone had any idea where he'd be going it'd be you!"

"Mrs. Braddock, I don't even think your son knows what's going on in his mind right now."

"What the hell is that supposed to mean?"

(Pause)

"Is he crazy?"

(Pause)

"Dr. Fuller? Dr. Fuller?"

"He's here."

"What?"

"Dan just walked into the institute."

# XIII

White. Its pigment is stark. It looks clean, so everything else in comparison or within the general vicinity of it looks sickly. Not bright or lively, as the notion always is. The hospital adorned the rooms in pure white, with the intention of giving a serene touch. Instead, a person pales next to the drab walls and the tiniest crack or mark in the white suddenly takes away the balance of the room. One is swept back into the reality that every object, including every person that inhabited the room at one instance, was damaged and broken.

The initial step into the hospital, as the sliding doors silently parted away from Dan, took him an exuberant amount of time. It was much longer than he anticipated, quite different from the image that he would briskly walk into the hospital, turn in his belongings and announce his name, stripping any outside world connection. But once he reached the building, watching the taxi out of the corner of his eye speed away as if he suddenly had the devil's numbers imprinted on his face, Dan realized that he stood in front of the building for minutes before his foot finally lifted off the ground. Once inside, a stale smell engulfed his nostrils, and a decaying hush fell over the scene, as if the whispers of the patients were being sucked clean from their lips. Dan had pictured this moment many times, but now that he was here, clutching to the bag at his side, he had no idea why he had originally pictured it the way he had. The image was that he would courageously walk straight to the front desk, be taken to his own room and have his mind rushed into simple-minded ease. There were no judgments, no questions, and no faltering steps.

That image seemed so unimaginable and juvenile now, like when a child experiences a funeral for the first time and has his eyes wide open to the true meaning of death. Here, it was the understanding that maybe there really was something wrong with him. The building was immense, old, and washed to a dull brown brick over the years. It looked strictly made for a mental institute, almost a set stage for a movie from decades ago, in which the patients cling to the iron bars of the windows or the ends of their beds, their faces plastered in fear or dulled by electric shock. The interior result harbored much different effects.

Modern renovations had cleaned the place of all the nasty reminiscences of past patients, the front entrance to the building be a recent renovation that screamed the message that the hospital was practicing modern science and medicine. *No electric shock here folks.* Nurses rushed in and out of the receding hallways, shutting doors while the locks automatically clicked. One standard security guard sat at the desk with the receptionist, a lanky woman whose hair was brushed firmly to her scalp and who barely glanced up from the papers she was reading. The ambience of the room was intended to relax a newcomer; but the plants that were placed strategically next to the huge windows and the shrill noises that echoed from the hallways, plastered in an ever-glowing white stripped any relaxing emotion that could quake through a person's bloodstream. Dan numbly walked up to the desk and opened his mouth.

"Dan," his mouth shut, he turned to his right and there stood Dr. Fuller. The man was tall, broadly built, and wore the strictly conservative suit and tie. His phone slipped into his pocket, his arm resting on the wooden reception desk. The receptionist hadn't even raised her head. "What are you doing here?"

"Well Doc, I just missed you so much—"

"Why did you not tell your parents?"

The icy glare that Dr. Fuller shot at Dan could have frosted the windows of the building, crystallizing all across the huge ceiling and walls. It was at this point that both the security guard and the receptionist noticed the middle aged doctor and disheveled college student standing in front of them.

"Was that them on the phone just then?" Dan's snide grin faded as he refused to meet Dr. Fuller's eye. Fuller stepped closer, bearing down on Dan as if he were an impudent child as opposed to a shell shocked twenty-some year old man.

"Yes Dan, that was your mother frantically calling me saying that her son was missing, nothing left behind to give any trace of where he might be and as I'm trying to assure her that you are alright you decide to waltz into my hospital. Why?"

The harsh fluorescent lights strained Dan's eyes. Pressing his fingers to his eyes did nothing to ease the pain, but rather punched bullets of color that whizzed in and out of his vision.

"You know why Doc," he affirmed dramatically. The eyes of the receptionist went from Dan who still avoided Fuller's look to the doctor himself, who had begun to drum his fingers against the counter in contemplation.

"You're here on your own accord, fully admitting yourself voluntarily?"

"Well there wasn't anyone else in the cab who wanted to join if that's what you're saying."

The drumming fingers ceased, his fist delicately bouncing off the counter. He nodded to the receptionist. An endless pool of questions poured out of her mouth, as Dan's identification and informal data were demanded. Fuller remained next to Dan the whole time, eyeing the boy's every hesitance; tweak and fumbled word.

"And why are you admitting yourself to the institution?"

Dan had placed a shaking hand over his mouth as he mumbled answers, and for a brief moment his hand stopped shaking, firmly gripping his chin.

"I'm here to protect my family."

"I'm going to need a more explicit answer than that."

Fuller clasped the folder that the receptionist had been writing in, scooping it into his hand and tucking it under his arm.

"It's alright Jean. I'll get him settled into a room and have him answer the last of the questions at our next session."

The receptionist dumbly allowed Fuller to take the folder, entering various amounts of information into the computer in front of her and completely shutting out the two men who stood in front of her once again. Fuller motioned for Dan to follow and turned towards the right hallway. A swipe of a card and Fuller swung the door open, revealing a white hallway that receded into another set of big metal doors, firmly shut with darkness following after. The bag at Dan's side knocked into the back of his leg, for a moment making his movements towards the hallway stiff and stilted. Fuller waited patiently as Dan apprehensively peered into the hallway. Not a soul moved.

"There's nothing here to pop out at you, I swear."

"No, I was just waiting for Nurse Ratched to appear."

Fuller shook his head as Dan finally walked past him, his tailored shoes clicking against the cold tile as they continued silently down the hall. The gray doors came closer and once again Fuller swiped his card, revealing an identical hallway to the one they just exited. To the left was a series of bared windows that gave way to an open courtyard which the building enclosed. To the right were dark green painted doors, each perfectly spaced apart from the other.

"You'll be living in this hall. You'll have your own room, shared bathroom."

"What? No tour."

Fuller stopped, grabbing Dan's jacket by the sleeve, spinning the boy around. His face was stern and not a hint of comfort was in his eyes.

"Not for people who decide that they need to come onto the grounds at two in the morning. No. You'll meet a nurse tomorrow who will show you around."

"Fine." Dan matched Fuller's severe glare, his eyes indignant and rattling with growing anger.

"This floor is minimal security Dan, which for your case should be fine. Don't make this more difficult than it needs to be. You know just as well as I do that you probably don't need to be here."

"Well, by the surprised look on your face when I walked in, you know just as well as I do that I probably do."

"Your coyness isn't going to be a winning defense mechanism Dan."

The two stood in the hallway with a cloud of seething discomfort and confrontation lashing out above them. The ticking of a nearby clock was overpowering, echoing in both of their eardrums like a timed bomb. Silently, with almost premeditated action, Fuller turned to the closest door. A ring of keys shinned in the light as they emerged from his coat pocket. He unlocked the door and swung it open. The room was small: one window, one bed, a dresser, and a small open closet. The furniture was a pale oak wood highlighted by the white walls. A set of worn blue curtains hung limply on either side of the window. The view from the window, apart from the white iron bars that one would have to peer through, yielded a view of the green area around Dan. No signs, no streets, no sounds of traffic.

"First rule, you're never allowed to have your door locked—"

"Why don't we just skip the rules for tonight, Doc."

Fuller stood momentarily in the doorway as Dan slowly walked his way through the small square room. His fingers traced every object, till finally he sat down on the bed with a great sigh as he dropped his bag.

"No one will be able to find me here, right?"

"No, besides your family, no one should even know that you're here."

"Jamie too. I'm going to tell her." Dan sat crouched over, staring at his hands as if they were not his own. Fuller flicked the keys back and forth in his hand with slight discomfort.

"Of course."

"I couldn't tell them, even before I left and knew that I was going to leave—"

"Why don't we save this for tomorrow, Dan."

Dan's head swiveled up to look at Fuller. The look on Dan's face suddenly aged him, as if he were returning from combat no longer a sprite young boy but a harden man.

"Sure thing, Doc."

"Good night Dan."

The door clicked shut. Dan was alone. He tentatively stood up, going towards the window. His fingers slid down the metal cage that barricaded Dan from the glass window, the iron bars and the open world. He was literally caged in; no one could get in or out. The surroundings around him, around the entire complex, hid them from view. He wasn't a student anymore, one who was constantly looking over his shoulder for someone to attack him. He wasn't a citizen of the world who refrained from the moral complexity of admitting to witnessing a murder. He would now be listed as the unstable adolescent male who couldn't take the pressure that society had thrown at him. So in effort to escape it, he came here. Was it really an escape though? His head rested on the cold metal, the tiny holes of the metal pattern imprinting on his forehead. Was this all really as messed up as he thought it was? He convinced himself again that all the events in the past couple of months were real, not the foggy dream that some people would have used an excuse and that his actions were plausible, if not the most practical. The scene was Jamie, and then men...that only confirmed the paranoia that began boiling up in his mind again. Here no one would find him. No one would look for him. He'd become the lore of the campus, for about a week people would question his disappearance from school. And then he'd be utterly forgotten. So then why did he still not feel safe?

"Hello?"

"Mom?"

"Dan!"

"Hey Ma."

"Dan, where are you?"

"I'm at the institute."

"Why? Dr. Fuller refuses to give us any more information besides saying that you're safe and where you need to be. What does he mean Dan? What's going on?"

"Ma..."

(Pause)

"Dan, please tell me."

"It's complicated."

"I don't care, Dan. One minute you're studying at school, acting as if nothing is wrong, the next you're checking yourself into a mental institute! Do you think you're crazy Dan?"

"It's not that Mom, there's more to it than that."

"Cause you're not crazy, you're not. Dan, I understand that you place yourself from everyone else and say that you're different, but there is no one on this earth who could convince me that something is wrong with you."

"Mom—"

"Your father and I are going to come visit you right away. And we're going to discuss with Dr. Fuller about releasing you as soon as possible."

"Mom, don't do that. It's not necessary."

"Yes it is, Dan, you don't need to be there."

"Mom—"

"Don't try to defend Dr. Fuller. He's being absolutely ridiculous."

"No he's not Mom."

"Yes he is. None of this is making any sense."

"I know Mom. I'm going to try to explain it to you, I swear."

"You shouldn't be there Dan!"

(Pause)

"Dan?"

(Pause)

"Yes, I should Mom."

"What?"

"I know that this is hard to hear Mom, but listen. I need to be here. I have my reasons; I know full well what I was doing when I checked myself in. This is the right decision, Mom. I…I won't be here long."

"Are they going to give you treatments, more medication? You don't need any of that—"

"Mom."

"This is insane—"

"Mom."

"I mean, you haven't done anything to prove any of this is necessary—"

"Mom."

(Pause)

"This is the right thing for me to do. Can you trust me on that?"

"When can we come visit you?"

"I don't want you visiting a lot?"

"Why not? Dan you're our son!"

"I know, I just...I wish I could explain more."

"Why can't you Dan?"

(Pause)

"I just...can't. Mom, I need you to promise me something."

"What?"

"Promise me that if anything ever looks suspicious, you tell the police right away."

"What do you mean Dan?"

"Just, if anyone drives by the house that normally doesn't, or if...I don't know Ma, just promise me that you, Dad, and Emily will be careful. Please promise me!"

"Of course Dan."

(Pause)

"Thank you."

"Will you not tell me anything Dan?"

(Pause)

"I have to go, I'm sorry Mom. For everything."

# XIV

Resilience. One definition says that of humans and animals, it is the ability to bounce back from difficult conditions. In regards to society today, it is a worthwhile quality to have within one's self. In an institution where they spoon feed questions, determine every action, and labor in every detail of a human that is marred, there are few who put up the resilient fight. Patients realize that in the end they are in more trouble than what they started with, and that putting up the "good fight" actually takes away privileges that one once had. In short, resilience is the only quality one wishes to not have in an institution. It is compliance that patients yearn for.

Dan knew from the start that he had too much resilience in him. Some tiny part of him, though most of his spirit had been broken down by the rapid deterioration of the life around him, made him strongly believe that every action he had taken after the event was with purpose, and that in the end it would all connect together like the surprising entertaining puzzle that sits in a living room. The compliance factor that he knew would speed up his recover and exit from the institutions was sorely lacking. The first night alone, he feigned sleep as a nurse walked past every so often and checked through the little window of his door to see that he was peacefully resting. He would hear her footsteps echoing down the hall, and position himself into an accurate portrayal of a young man sleeping. Once the hall became silent, suddenly his was body was contorted again with rigid precision as thoughts still gripped his mind and paranoia still raked through to his fingertips that wrung the bed sheets at his side.

Compliance was far from his mind. He knew the system; he knew what it took to get him out of here. And in the feeble comfort that he briefly felt every so often in the small room that he had been confined in, he realized that resilience would keep him here, but would also keep up the motivation for something greater than just the attempt at the profound idea that every citizen in the world could be brought back into some form of sanity.

The first morning, he was rudely awoken by the knock on a door, as a nurse popped her head to announce breakfast. Like a grumpy child, he lumbered into the common room, immediately being led to take medications. The pills sat still in the curled palm of his hand, and his eyebrows cringed.

"Why do I need to take these?"

"They will help calm you down." The response was quick and then he was shoved aside as the next patient in line came up to the window.

"Didn't know I was acting up." The pills landed on his tongue, but no matter how much he tried, he couldn't muster them down. A swish of water, and then the euphoria of the drug hit. Dan spent the entire first day sitting on an old couch, watching from the corner as patients scattered about.

Some barely spoke, some hardly moved, staring into the space that Dan every once in a while found in the center of the room. Some screamed, their bodies rigid, as a nurse and security led them back to their rooms. Some mumbled inaudible tunes that were the harmonies to the symphony of the fans that buzzed in each ceiling corner of the room. Dan sat dazed, wearily looking from one person to other, finding himself sinking further and further into the couch as discomfort grew. He retreated to his room, but it was no better, since he was utterly alone to his own thoughts. He curled into his bed, his knees up to his face in a defeated fetal position.

Day one.

Day two marked the beginning of the growing fight. Dan sat waiting in Fuller's office, a grand room that marked every single penny that the man had earned in his lifetime. The huge window revealed a sparkling, picturesque view of the grounds, as opposed to the gray branches that covered most of the patients' windows. Bookcases filled with large expensive texts adorned two of the walls. The chairs were fine leather, the edges finally wearing down from years of patients rubbing their fingers back and forth on the ends of the arms nervously. The wooden desk was polished, not a trace of dust littered on it, with office items that one pictured on every desk, as if Fuller were advertising his office for a catalogue. Dan sat in amusement, the medications from the first day finally wearing off, today's dose tucked away in his sock, the only place he could store them before leaving for Fuller's office.

The door swung open and Fuller walked in, holding a file close to his face as he sidestepped by Dan. He had been here only two days and the hospital had a file, an entire file dedicated to the life of a boy who wanted nothing more than a diploma and a pitch perfect life. The inexplicit way that Fuller flipped through the file told Dan that they really had nothing at all on him. But he sat still in the armchair, anticipating the first session. Fuller sat in the chair opposite of him, closed the file, and looked up at Dan with almost a gleeful smile on his face, as if this were his greatest joy in life.

"How are you doing today Dan?"

"Fine."

"That was a very reassuring fine."

"Well I'm feeling pretty sure about it." Fuller hadn't moved from his position of power. He didn't hold onto a notebook, only a fancy pen between his fingers as if he held all the answers in the world with every line of ink that poured out of the pen. But still, the way he sat in the chair, leaning comfortably against the back of it while Dan squirmed at every moment created a sustained unease in the room, even after the first words had been spoken.

"So is this how it will be Dan? We've been talking and having sessions for months. Nothing's changed." Dan looked at Fuller with an incredulous look.

"You're really going to try and get away with saying that? That nothing's changed? I'm in a hospital!"

"So, let's talk about that." Dan's jaw clenched and he picked a stained spot on the carpet to continuously stare at for torturous silent minutes.

"The silent treatment isn't going to work forever,    Dan." Dan glared up with a look that said *"Wanna bet?"* Fuller sighed.

"Have you talked to your parents since you came here?"

"No."

"Jamie?" Dan cocked his head, eyebrows raised. Fuller gulped down the derision that he wished to throw at the young man, waiting for a reply before hastily making his counterargument.

"What do you think?"

"I'll take that as a no then." Dan nodded, his eyes traveling to all corners of the office. Fuller followed his gaze as Dan's eyes fell onto the view from the window, the books, and the photos that were scattered amongst the many volumes of text throughout the office.

"So what's the procedure Doc? I come in here every day and we just talk?"

"Yes, that's pretty much it. We can reevaluate everything that has happened: your goals and what you want to get out of your stay here, possible solutions to help the situation, what you plan to do once you get out…"

"Why would we want to reevaluate everything? That seems like a moot point." Dan's eyes sparked with unkindness at the idea of revisiting every single image that had tormented him for the past few months of his life.

"Well, it can serve as a start." Fuller explained, trying to provide reassurance. Dan had begun picking at the worn leather of the chair, his fingers grazing every edge of the arm.

"Do you want to start there?" The young man across from Fuller didn't respond. "Dan? I need to get some answer from you at some point in this session."

Dan repositioned himself on the chair, moving away from Fuller towards the window. His eyes glazed over as he stared at the leaves rustling in the wind and heard the sound of a car starting and driving away. His body had completely molded into the chair, yet Fuller still glanced down at Dan's foot, which was unceasingly and relentlessly tapping disturbingly against the ground.

"Dan?"

"I don't want to talk today."


Day two.

---

Day three marked another day that Dan tried to sneak away his medication, but the nurse evidently had a note from Fuller indicating the lack of dosage within Dan's system, and therefore cautiously watched Dan until he finally slipped the pills into his mouth and washed it down with the small glass of water. His session with Fuller that afternoon was more progressive in Fuller's eyes. Dan fumbled with questions, but nevertheless was an open book to Fuller that day. And Dan found himself unable to fight the feeling that itched inside him, the need to have every question that was on his mind answered. The images had faded from his memory that day, he hardly saw the girl that night when he slept, but he still was able to discuss it, and with an exasperated enthusiasm.

"How are you feeling today, Dan?"

"Better, but then again the drugs you keep giving me might have a little to do with that."

"The drugs should help you Dan. They help keep you calm."

"Will they help me forget?" The desperate look in Dan's eyes made Fuller hesitate. Today he had issued himself a notebook, writing down quick lines that focused on Dan's behavior and the topics of conversation.

"Well, the medication itself won't, Dan. But that's why I'm here. To help you cope."

Dan nodded, as if that were the best and most reliable answer he had heard his whole life. His arms hung off each end of the chair, his fingers curled but still shaking, as if the boy had dosed himself with absorbent amounts of caffeine.

"Do you think I'm crazy Doc?" Fuller paused, looking directly at the patient in front of him. Dan's eyes still held the desperate look, like a lost pet that finally found its way home.

"That's the first time you ever asked a question that truly deals with the situation at hand, Dan. Plus my opinion in earnest."

"Great, so answer it before I change my mind on the whole fixing me thing." Dan's fingers had begun a tug of war on each other, his nails digging into the tips of the opposite hand's fingers.

"No Dan, I don't think you're crazy. I think you are part of the sometimes unbelievable phenomenon that when a person witnesses violence they have a hard time forgetting about it. Many people think that it would be easy, but most of the time these are the people that will never witness something like this ever in their lives. I think that you need some help. But there is no doubt in my mind that you could go back out into society and live a very normal life Dan."

"What if they find me? The people that killed her. What if they want to kill me too?" Sweat had begun to pool at his forehead, tiny beads that welled up at the edge of his hairline, though his breathing was steady. The deep seeded paranoia that Dan had accustomed for himself still was apparent.

"Why have you never considered the police, Dan? If you could describe the men, describe what happened they probably would be able to find the men if they haven't already. You really have nothing to worry about."

Dan wildly shook his head the whole time Fuller suggested going to the police.

"If I go to the cops then they will have all my information. If the guys killed her find out then they can come to my house, kill my family."

"How would they find out your information Dan?"

"In questioning. The cops could walk away for a split second, the guys memorize my address from where it sits on the cop's desk.

They come to my house after denying everything, I mean they are murderers; they probably have a decent alibi. People like this always plan ahead, cause they know that something could happen." Fuller watched the entire fantasy spill from Dan's mouth. The vivid imagination that had concocted the whole scene in Dan's head was incredible.

"Dan," Fuller began with a consoling tone. "If any of that were true, which in your case is very slim to none in actually happening, the cops would know right away that you and your family would be a group of people that they would immediately want to protect. Dan, the chances of any of that ever happening—"

"But it could, right? I mean, we're not trying to figure out the odds of all the different scenarios. The fact is, even if it's some slim chance, this could happen! It's possible! At least tell me that Doc, that it's all possible." Dan had leaned forward, reaching for Fuller as if reaching for confirmation. His arms were held out in midair, his fingers curling into fists. Fuller opened his mouth, and then closed it. He had during this whole time written down verbatim everything that Dan had said. The tape recorder at his side would later confirm that the boy's frantic nature was real, not just part of Fuller's imagination.

"Of course Dan, it could be possible." Fuller couldn't believe that he was feeding into the delusion that Dan had created. But for a moment, he couldn't think of anything else to do to help the poor soul in front of him. Dan slumped back into his seat, as if he had just fought of a fit of fever. He cradled his head in his hands, which glistened with perspiration.

"I just want to protect them. They have nothing to do with this."

"I know Dan."

Day three.

---

Day four and Dan woke up angry. At first he didn't know what it was, he couldn't quite pinpoint what had set him off. The medication had worn off, and the startling dependence that Dan had gained towards the medication was signaled by the pounding headache. He sat curled in his bed, seething with anger because of everything that Fuller had managed to pump out of him yesterday, and yearning for nothing more than another dose of the pills to make him feel better, but that thought only made him punch his pillow in frustration. He couldn't fall to them now, falter like a broken glass off a table after only four days. He didn't want to be dependent on this hospital; it was the last place that he wanted to be today.

Fuller was already standing when Dan walked in to the office, as if completely aware of the growing distain that gathered in the hallway as Dan walked closer, a gathering storm that was finally bearing down on him. The pills were tucked in Dan's hand, which had slipped quite surreptitiously past the nurse and directly for Fuller's office, opening the door and slamming it. The two men stood facing each other, both poised for the growing fight ahead.

"What changed Dan?" Fuller began.

"Don't pull that psychological crap with me Doc!" Dan threw the pills to the ground, his head raging and pounding. "Screw that medication. It makes me feel like shit and completely compliant to everything anyone says to me, like I'm some lab rat."

"That's not why we're giving you the medications Dan. We're not trying to control you. It's supposed to help you." Fuller had slipped behind the armchair that was next to his desk, using the furniture as a barrier between him and Dan, who still stood fuming with fists clenched.

"Cut the shit Doc! There is no 'we'! It's just you and me, like it's always been!" Dan walked to the middle of the room, a sturdy stance making him immovable. Fuller remained where he was behind the chair, gripping the pen that was in his palm, legitimately weary of the young man in front of him.

"What happened, Dan?"

"You happened! All of this shit happened!" His feet began pacing the room, his hands on either side of his forehead as he tried to figure out the exact words to say, weeding through the needles of pain that shot through his head. "My life was fine before all of this shit. It's too much now! I'm fucking sick of life being interesting! I…" Dan faltered, his hands drooping in defeat. His eyes closed and he took a deep breath. "I never wanted any of this." Anger still swayed in his eyes that had locked onto Fuller. The pen that Fuller had wound amongst his fingers was warm, the ink boiling as much as the minds of the two men in the room. "I was fine before all of this. And now? I can't get her face out of my mind. I can't walk past that damn alley without seeing the whole entire scene over again. This whole time it's been a terrible nightmare, even from the beginning. And it never leaves. I can't get it to leave." His voice quaked and his hands began to shake as they clenched and unclenched. He looked back up at Fuller. "I'm not crazy Doc," he whispered.

Fuller inched away from the chair, stepping closer to the middle of the room. Dan seemed to shrink back, as if the pen in Fuller's hand were a weapon. "I'm not crazy," he repeated with a feeble voice.

"Dan, you're right. You're not crazy. But you do need help," Fuller dropped his voice to the softest level he could manage, hoping that Dan would eventually sit down, or even better, finally calm down. But Dan was too agitated. His body was like a sheet of glass that could shatter at any second.

"I shouldn't be here Doc." Fuller stopped the defensive argument and suddenly began to freeze in his tracks. "This place is driving me nuts and I've been here four days. There are people out there who rock back and forth even though they're not sitting in a chair. There are people talking to nothing, as if they were best of friends. I'm not like them! I'm not that crazy person who drools because he's so doped on medications, who's so cut away from reality. I shouldn't fucking be here Doc!"

"Then why did you come here, Dan? Nobody forced you to walk into the hospital and check yourself in that night Dan. You have no one to blame for this but yourself."

A clap of thunder, and the storm had begun.

"Fuck you Doc! You're the one who keeps on saying that I need help, yet you haven't helped me one bit."

"Oh, and I suppose you're going to say that Jamie is helping you more than me. You haven't talked to her in days Dan! I'm all you've got right now!"

"Well, I don't want you!"

"That's too damn bad, Dan. You made that decision when you walked in here!"

"There wasn't any other place I could go! I needed to get away from my house. And there was no way in hell you could convince me to go back to that damn school!"

"So what do you plan to do about it, Dan? You only have a few options, and trust me, you probably won't like them."

"Get me out of here!" Dan had taken two steps, and in the matter of space that he had covered suddenly he was only a foot away from Fuller. The two stood too close for comfort, but neither made the effort to move back.

"I can't do that, Dan. You have to prove that you don't need to be here."

"But I don't need to be here!"

"You're right, and I know that," Fuller said. Dan backed away with a confused look plastered on his face. "But you don't believe that. A part of you knows that you need my help. You need that to have that feeling that you have a purpose again Dan, and you can't get that by working on your own. And you know that."

Silence clung to every inch of the room. And with a breath, Fuller watched Dan finally fade into the background, slipping into the white of the walls behind him. It was a victory for Fuller, but the defeat that suddenly overtook Dan took with it his fire.

"Screw you Doc." He walked towards the door, stepping on the pills he had discarded before and snapping them open, the white powder spilling from them into the carpet. The Door swung open and slammed, Dan was gone. Fuller sat in his chair, taking a huge sigh before resting his head in his hands.

"Hello?"

"Jamie?"

"Dan?"

"I have a phone call for the night. They think I'm calling my parents, but you were the only person I really wanted to talk to."

(Pause)

"How are you Dan?"

(Pause)

"I don't know."

"What are they doing? It's not like electric shocks or anything, is it?"

"No Jamie. They're giving me medications, but it's the same stuff as before. I hate it. It doesn't make me feel right."

"So stop taking it."

"Some days I can, others they watch me like hawks."

"How long are you going to stay there?"

"I don't know."

"Well, they can't keep you there forever. Plus it's not like you're actually crazy."

(Silence)

"Dan?"

"I do need help Jamie."

"Yeah, help as in transfer to a new school, stick with friends and

153

family who will help you get over it."

"Doc says I should go to the police."

"Why in God's name would you do that?"

"The police could help."

(Pause)

"You don't think I should, do you?"

"Not at all."

"I just don't want them to find my family."

"If you went to the police and they found these guys, that's exactly what could happen. They easily could figure out where you live Dan."

"I know."

"Why take that risk at all?"

"I know."

"Can I visit?"

"No. Just my family."

"What if I come anyways? I still don't get why they are keeping you at that place Dan. You're not crazy."

(Pause)

"Dan?"

"I have to go. I'll talk to you soon."

# XV

Time is a funny thing. When one has an enormous list, a copious amount of things that need to get finished within a certain period of time, the minutes speed past with a moment's glance. The end comes sooner than one wants it, and the incredible feeling of dread sets in as one tries desperately to finish everything in the allotted amount of time. When one doesn't need the time, it slows down to a sluggish pace, like a traffic jam that one can't escape from. One sits and waits impatiently, flicking a pen against a notebook, watching the minutes slowly tick away as if each one were suddenly longer than sixty seconds. The solution to both of these problems of course is society's will to measure and control time; bend it according to their own lives.

So what about the person who literally doesn't care about time, the apathetic person who could watch time slip through his fingers, or watch it pace slowly behind him in the marathon to the end? Does this person really have control over time, or has he broken himself away from the system completely, as if watching time from an entirely different plane?

The two-week mark had finally approached, and Dan realized as he trudged to Fuller's office that he honestly didn't care. He wasn't angry about the fact that he was a healthy child locking himself up in a mental institute, but at the same time he utterly wasn't happy about it either. His mind had clouded over, a fogged conscious that wasn't clinging to any hope, nor had succumbed to the feeling of miserable failure. He simply trudged on, from room to room; obeying the orders that were thrown at him because he had no reason not to; and still he dreamed every night about the murder because he had no energy to fight it anymore. In a sick method, it had become a part of him. It was a fantasy that taunted his mind every night. For a brief moment when he awoke, he assured himself that it had all been a dream. And then his fingers brushed the crisp white sheets and his eyes gazed onto the white wash walls. From the sweat that pooled around his face, and the breaths that heaved his chest up and down every day as he woke with a start, his mind knew that figuratively he could create the whole scenario off as a hellish nightmare, that none of it was reality. But when reality becomes even as grave as dreams, what's the point?

He stepped up to the great wooden door, his knuckles rapping against it. Silence responded. Dan knocked again, only to have the room whisper back that no one was in. He turned the knob, and the door swung open with ease. The office was empty. Tiny lines of sunlight peeked in through the blinds, leaving oddly angled patterns all along the floor. Dan paused in the doorway, and then walked in without a remorseful thought. Dan couldn't exactly explain what gravitated him to the center of the office. If someone were to have asked him he would say it was an extraordinary force that willed him to where the lines of sunlight suddenly slashed onto his skin. The sun warmed his arms as he stood staring out the window, the lines highlighting every imperfection on his arm, even the tiniest bruise and crease in his skin. For a second, his mind went back to the childhood scene when a boy kills ants with the magnify glass, burning the little creatures into tiny crisps that easily float away with a wind that draws across the sidewalk. The image of a huge magnifying glass coming up to the window appeared in Dan's mind. He wondered if he were an ant, would anyone brush him aside, or just step on him as they continued to walk on the sidewalk.

"Dan. Good morning." Fuller entered his open door, looking down at the ever-growing manila folder that held the sticker with Dan's name on the tab. He solemnly closed the door to his office, ignoring the fact that Dan had entered without permission, and calmly walked to his desk and sat down; taking a minute more to read some notes and then closing the folder quite strategically. In the whole process Dan followed Fuller's movements, taking one small step towards the man's desk, and standing like an obedient child.

"Learning anything new Doc?" he asked. Fuller, head still bent, glanced up at Dan. A small smile crooked along his face. Dan uncomfortably shifted on his feet, his fingers inching into his jean pockets, tugging at the cotton fabric inside.

"As I matter a fact I have Dan."

"Really? So what's the good word?" Fuller motioned for Dan to take a seat, following suite and taking his proper place across from his patient. The two sat, the interminable gaze between them heating up. Dan sat stiffly while Fuller collapsed as if a college boy who had finally finished a day's worth of class. The role reversal between their body language was astonishing, as if Dan were the nervous doctor who was interviewing the passive boy.

"Did you think I wouldn't notice Dan?"

"What are you talking about Doc?" Fuller sighed; reaching behind him for the folder he was just reading, dramatically opening it and flipping through white pages that contained line after line of black inked words.

"Completely compliant, takes medication, participates in discussion, etcetera," Fuller spoke with a condescending rasp, his voice dripping with the elusive doubt he held towards Dan. Dan's jaw clenched, looking out towards the window. A single twinge marked the boy's growing impatience. "On paper, you're almost perfect."

"Great," the snide remark came out faster than Dan thought. He refused to look at Fuller, his eyes searing as he looked out the window. The sun still streaked the floor of the office. *What I'd give for that magnifying glass right about now.* "So, what's the problem then?" Fuller leaned forward in his chair, the folder idly held in one hand indignantly, as if every bit of information contained within the file only made Dan more and more incriminating.

"I don't believe it."

A cloud came across the sky, a shadow falling across the floor of the office. Dan still was unable to look at Fuller; the man's face only sparked the disdain that Dan continually tried to hide from the man.

"Surprise, surprise." The folder slammed onto the table in between them, miraculously flipping open as if someone had waved a magic wand, going directly to the pages that begun the words of praise towards Dan. Dan glanced at it between his fingers; his hand cradling his jaw and hiding his grinding teeth. He switched positions, sitting cavalier in the chair. Oppositely, Fuller sat upright, his chest welling with pride.

"Why don't you think I believe you Dan?"

"Because I remind you of yourself as a child," Dan's quip was accompanied with a smile as Dan sat lazily in the chair, his eyes slanted up towards Fuller with an egotistical gaze. Fuller's tongue could be seen running along his teeth, his lips bulging out for a split second before a chuckle broke his lips. His fingers were placed in front of him, the contemplative look that every doctor gave their patient. Dan sat unfazed; one leg sprawled over the leg, his eyes unmoving.

"Snide comments aren't going to get you out Dan."

"Damn and they always say charm can get you so far in life."

"I don't believe you because two weeks ago every single day you showed a different emotion. One day you were sacred out your mind, the other you came into this office with the intention of beating me to a pulp; that's how angry you were. And then suddenly, two weeks later, you are as compliant as a patient who's had a full frontal lobotomy. Tell me Dan, did you really think faking it all would get you out of here faster?"

The sunlight was shining through the window again. The lines began small, and as they drew closer to the men only grew wider, but more unfocused. The closer an object comes to someone, the more unclear it becomes. To look at the beginning of the shadows, when so far away from the actual object, it seems clear as day. Step closer, and the world disengages, falls apart at one's fingertips like decaying cloth. Step closer, and one can't decipher a thing, the answer's too far away to grasp.

" 'Of some, no memory survives the instant of their passage. Of others, it is confined to a few moments, hours or days. Others again, leave vestiges which are indestructible, and by means of which they may be recalled as long as life endures'."

Fuller leaned forward in his chair, a look of empathy on his face. Dan turned away from the striped shadows on the floor, looking directly at the man sitting in front of him.

"William James."

"A plus Doc."

A pen emerged into Fuller's hand. His fingertips brushed along each end, and then it was unwilling struck against the palm of his opposite hand. A ceaseless drumming began, the pen bouncing dully against the taunt skin of Fuller's hand, the non-hollow palm yielding almost no sound at all, but if one listened carefully, it could be heard.

"Are you still having nightmares?" Dan nodded.

"Still seeing her face?" A second nod.

"Will it ease your mind to hear that this is proof for me. Proof that you're not just trying to be compliant, but are actually trying to work on getting better."

"You mean coping."

"Coping is sometimes the best method for people in dealing with things in this world."

The pen stopped. No matter how many times he could beat it against his hand, it still distilled the same answer.

"Can I ask you another question Dan?"

"Why not?"

"Have you talked to Jamie recently?"

Dan turned away, retreating back towards the window.

"She's a trigger, Dan." Dan's head spun back around, his

brow furrowed, his mouth hanging open with words latched to the end of his lips, but with no method of releasing themselves.

"Every time she's mentioned, it comes with a heavy emotion, whether it is sadness or anger. It also comes with an intense recollection of that night, and you know it. Without Jamie—"

"She has nothing to do with that night."

"Without Jamie, you've been progressing in a positive way Dan."

"Twenty minutes you didn't have any faith in me at all."

"There's a lot you can learn in twenty minutes, Dan."

Dan scoffed, crossing his arms across his chest as his body slumped down into the chair. Fuller placed the pen on top of the folder that was on the table. The folder closed with a quiet whoosh of air, and then was grasped by Fuller's hand and laid in his lap.

"Just take it into consideration, the people that can help you Dan, and those that only hinder from forgetting." A cold stare shot at Fuller.

"There's no forgetting, Doc."

"I'm sorry; I didn't mean it like that. I only meant that in getting better, in learning to deal with this, think of what you can let go."

Dan licked his lips in fervent discomfort, his eyes trailing back up towards Fuller, who waited patiently, but Dan knew of nothing else to say. Silently, the young man stood up, and with feigned determination walked out of the office back towards the room.

Dan knew immediately walking back to his room that something was awry. It was in the way the hospital looked. Dusk and fallen and the last bits of light that peeked in throughout all the great windows cast shadows that danced and floated along the shiny tile floors. Everything could suddenly become ethereal amongst the dim light. The branches were suddenly long spiny fingers, the curtains hiding the cleverest of objects that for a split second could suddenly look like a person lurking but in reality was only a nightstand. Dan quickly opened the doors to the hall where his room sat, the shadows that leaned against his door shifting ever so slightly. His fingers grazed the cold doorknob, a shiver running down his spine. He turned the knob and opened the door.

"Hi Dan."

A shadowed figure stood in front of his window, inches from his bed. He flicked the lights on, her blond hair cascading down her back.

"Jamie?" She turned at the sound of her name. She wore only plain clothes, a simple jacket, but still she electrified the whole room. She stood calmly, nonchalantly and Dan just as imperturbably closed the door behind him. "How did you get in here?"

A small sad smile crept to her lips as she stepped forward, but Dan took a step back. She stopped, her brow crinkling in disappointment, her big eyes looking away.

"I told them I was your sister. I can leave if you want. I just…I just wanted to see you."

Dan considered her face, the way it was held, and the way her eyes would meet his and then look away. Her body inched closer and the electricity between the two people standing in the room jumped from one end to the other, unceasingly thrilling. Dan still had yet to say anything, and when he stepped closer to her words caught in his throat as she looked up at him with a longing gaze. He sidestepped, his legs buckling him down onto his bed. Jamie turned and remained where she was, her head cocked to one side as she tried to meet his eyes, but Dan had gone to grinding his teeth, his fingers wringing themselves in and out of his palms. The grinding sound, the sheer force of Dan crunching his teeth against one another in elevated anxiety was the only sound in the room for some minutes.

Once he finally gathered up the courage to look at her again, her face was different. The darkness from outside had shadowed her face. Her eyes suddenly seemed to have sunken in, her cheeks more hollowed than he remembered. And the light that at one moment made her eyes shine had all but extinguished every breath of life that was in her face. She was a ghost, a quieter soul than Dan recalled. She wasn't the same.

"You shouldn't be here Jamie." His words grated against her skin. She stepped closer and he shrank back.

"You shouldn't be either." She gingerly sat down on the edge of the bed. Her face still looked vacant, her eyes searching Dan's face for answers but he couldn't give her any. "How are you?" Dan looked over at her, the genuine tone that came out of her voice filling his mind with guilt for avidly avoiding her. The two sat, a pair that held the same exhausted position, feeble breaths tugging at each of their chests. Something still stirred between them, but wouldn't make it in the dreary world that Dan had fabricated for himself.

"I'll be fine."

"Will you?" Her stare was fixated and Dan couldn't escape it. He stared straight back at her, and knew that the words that came out of his mouth were an utter lie, but it was all that he could say.

"Eventually, yes I will be."

"Come back to school Dan," her plea was fervent. "Please."

"I can't." Dan fought back. "Not yet." Jamie nodded, finally acceding to Dan's evasion. For minutes neither spoke a word. Dan stared off in the emptiness of his room, while Jamie ever so often would glance over at him. Her eyes still looked sunken in, all emotion being sucked dry from them. Tentatively, she reached over, placing her hand on his shoulder, squeezing it to signal her support. Dan quickly stood up, her hand numbly falling beside her.

"You can't come back here Jamie." She stood up abruptly, for a split second her eyes glistened with anger.

"Why not?" She wanted the fight, just in order to get any sort of feeling out of Dan. He still had his back turned to her, willing her to walk out the door without another word. "Dan!"

"Because you're not supposed to be here, Jamie." He spun around to face her. His face was masked in distress. It wasn't a frown on his face, nor tears in his eyes. It was rather a face completely dislodged of emotion, with one fleeting apology coming from his eyes before they became cold and lifeless to the situation. Jamie stood in disbelief.

"What is that supposed to be mean?"

"Just promise you won't come back here Jamie. Please." She shook her head, willing herself not to hear the words that Dan said. "If there's anything you can do for me, don't come back here."

Dan watched as her body slumped forward from where she sat, her face buried by her long hair. Then she raised her face to look at him; likewise he looked down and watched her unchanging expression. Their eyes held an intense look, but the scenario didn't change. Fuller's advice echoed throughout Dan's mind, and he knew that the instant Jamie walked out the door he was losing her. *Guess it's the price to pay...*

"Fine." And then she was gone. Dan sat down on the bed where she had been moments before, waiting for the click of her heels to fade away. His body then folding over onto the bed, his body curled up into a fetal position. The shadows from the trees danced on his cheeks as the wind lulled them back and forth, but his eyes were unwavering from the dark spot in the corner of the room where they sat.

"This is Dr. Fuller."

"Hello Dr. Fuller, its Mrs. Braddock."

"Yes, hello Mrs. Braddock, what can I do for you?"

"Well, my husband and I were wondering when we could come visit Dan."

(Pause)

"I see."

"Dan's been there for two weeks, and minus the updates that we get from you, which frankly are very vague and unclear, we haven't heard from him at all."

"Well, Dan has phone privileges. Has he not been calling you?"

"No, he hasn't."

"Interesting."

"How so?"

"He's strictly allowed to call only his family."

"Who would he be calling instead?"

"It doesn't matter."

"Dr. Fuller, please when can we come visit?"

"With Dan's case and I'd say that you'd be able to visit next week."

"Alright."

(Pause)

"Visiting is on Sunday afternoons. You and your family are

welcome to come next week to see Dan."

"Thank you."

(Pause)

"Is there anything else I can do for you Mrs. Braddock?"

"How is he, really?"

"He's doing very well."

"I didn't want the friendly small talk that you give all the parents Dr. Fuller."

"You sound just like him, Dan."

"Oh?"

"I meant only that you would fight to get what you want."

"That's correct, so where's my answer Dr. Fuller."

(Pause)

"Dan is progressing. He's still in need of help getting over what is troubling him—"

"And what exactly is troubling him Dr. Fuller?"

"I'm not the one to say that."

"I don't care if technically you're not allowed, I want to know."

"I meant that Dan should be the one to tell you, not me."

(Pause)

"Is it serious?"

(Pause)

"Though it could be damaging for some, I feel personally that Dan is strong enough to cope with this, and get his life back in order."

"Is he in danger?"

"Only if he thinks he is, Mrs. Braddock."

(Silence)

"Mrs. Braddock?"

"Thank you Dr. Fuller. I will see you next week."

# XVI

*He was running; It was either that or he was barely breathing. A labor-induced sweat covered his entire body. Beads of sweat coursed down his arms, weaving paths to the ends of his fingertips, where they dangled for moments before falling. An unceasing pounding rang in his ears, muffling the thousands of voices that engulfed him. It was a quiet drone of voices; as if his sense of hearing was slowly being ripped from him. The pounding continued as the slight tinkling of piano keys. But the sound wasn't light and jovial. It was harsh, a single finger bashing the same key over and over again until Dan wanted to scrape at the inside of his head if it meant stopping the sound. He ran, but there was no path. He heard distant sounds, but they never drew closer. His chest heaved to the rhythm of the piano keys. Even when he paused, took a deep breath, his heart still raced. And there was nothing around him. He reached down to the ground that his feet were planted on. His fingers scrapped against the cold gravel that disintegrated at his touch, yet there was residue on his fingertips.*

*He spun around, and a shadowed figure stood there. He shouted at it but it didn't back away in fright. He took a giant step forward, yet it didn't shrink back. The two stood face-to-face as the droned voices faded. The two stood in utter silence. Dan felt his finger twitch, the shadow's head moved. Suddenly the piano's keys were roars. The voices were deep seeded cries that finally broke free from captivity.*

*A flash of red.*

*"Dan!"*

"Dan…Dan." Fuller watched as the boy sprang awake, his body uncurling from the feeble position as he groaned sitting up.

"You're parents are here Dan, they're waiting in the lobby." Dan rubbed sleep from his eyes, his body shivering from the cold air that rammed into him when he shook the covers off. Fuller stood upright, rigidly walking back to the door of Dan's room. With hesitance, he turned back around as Dan climbed out of bed, grabbing a clean shirt.

"As a suggestion, today might be a good day to tell them."

"Why?" Dan turned back around. What surprised the older man was that it wasn't a look of anger, but rather Dan looked perturbed. It was like trying to reveal a harbored secret that up until now had all but defined the boy's life. Take away the secret, and with it went the idea of identity. "What's so special about today that makes it a good day?"

"Just a suggestion, take it or leave it." Dan provided no response as he finished changing into a new set of clothes. Fuller waited patiently, indicating the hallway.

"Ready?"

"What is this, part of you big plan?" Dan quipped as he brushed past Fuller, expanding the distance between him as the doctor as much as he could.

To picture, if it's possible, a scene in which parents visit their son in an institution. Do they smile? Do they laugh? When they finally see their son, will he look different?  Changed? Furthermore, and perhaps this is the greatest question: should the parents act as if nothing is wrong with their son? Or should they acknowledge that perhaps deep down there is a malfunctioning chord that is harming their son, strumming in the opposite beat as the rest of his body? After all, the conversation one always has during a visit is civil, as if nothing is wrong. But is that right?

Dan's parents thought about nothing else as they drove to the institute, walked in and waited as Fuller went to grab their son. The thought alone that someone had to escort Dan around caused both of them to stand on edge as they waited as patiently as their minds could allow. Minutes sluggishly ticked by, seconds appeared in the form of minutes. Dan's parents were looking from one thing to the next, to the nurse who carelessly clipped papers to a clipboard and then walked away; to the orderly who was escorting a patient slowly back to his room. The vacant expression that was plastered on the patient's face made Dan's mother clamp his father's hand tightly, fearing to let go in case one could get sucked into sickly monotony of lives that the patients lived.

The doors swung open and Fuller stood in the center of the doorway, ushering Dan's parents to follow. They met in a small room close to Dan's room. It was open, spacious, with a huge window that overlooked the grounds. It was a sort of meeting space one could predict, the air smelled of cleanliness. There were the strategically placed cups for coffee, while the idle coffee maker sat in the corner on top of the worn countertops. The chairs and furniture was new, a table to the side containing issued magazines that bore news about the latest fashion trends, home decorating styles and fishing equipment, yet they had become obsolete in the days that they spent splayed across the table for no one to read. Fuller entered the room, followed by the parents.

Upon entrance, both were able to place their eyes on their son, this being the first time in a matter of three weeks. They had imagined him to look so much more different than he did. He hadn't lost much weight; the bags of exhaustion that had previously clouded his face had disappeared. He wore the same clothes that had fitted him for years, and he still rocked back and forth uncomfortably for a few seconds, before settling on leaning forward with his hands wringing themselves back and forth in each other, as if he were extinguishing every last drop of moisture from his skin. But there was something that they both saw when he looked away from the window and finally back at them. His eyes were wider, more concerned and older. The way that he looked them up and down, they could have easily just been bystanders on the street that he had seen from the bench that he had been sitting at. It was the indifference to the scene around him, the meeting itself, that made his parents sit down with trepidation across from him.

"Hi guys."

"Hi honey, how are you doing?" His mom reached over, her hand resting on Dan's. Dan gave a small smile, his lips parting stiffly before he moved his hands, laying back into the chair. His mom's hand hovered awkwardly in the air between the two couches, and then she slowly reeled it back towards her, as if her hand carried some disease all over it.

Fuller grabbed a chair and set it at the head of the two couches, a notepad in hand. He took a deep breath as he sat, exhaling only after shuffling open his folder and notebook and taking his pen, placing it squarely between his two fingers firmly.

"Dan's made a lot of progress over the past three weeks. He's been sleeping more and eating pretty regularly. Our sessions have been going well, too. Wouldn't you say Dan?" Three pairs of eyes fell onto Dan. His fingers curled, his skin turning a snow white from where his nails dug into his own hand. The three pairs of eyes glanced away, and the fingers unclenched.

"You seem to be reporting just fine on my condition Doc." Fuller's lips were strained as he frowned slightly, giving Dan a sigh and an uplifted eyebrow that Dan equally returned with a condescending gleam in his eye.

"Is he still taking the meds?" His dad broke the silence, but nothing was going to tear down the wall that Fuller and Dan had begun building up. The two stared at each other with stern unresolved glares.

"Why don't you ask me, Dad," Dan's head swiveled over to face his father. "Huh?" His eyes held that same disagreement with Fuller, but now aimed at his parents.

"You're not the doctor, are you?"

"No, but he's not the one taking the meds." Fuller leaned forward, intervening on the cumulating degree of strain that was working its way into the room. Dan's mother was pretending to ignore the harsh tones in the diatribe between father and son.

"He is still on medications. But I feel that they are helping him. It's a very low dosage and it's helping keep him stable."

"Stable?" Fuller choked on the next of his words, a cough emanating from his mouth in order to cover up the degree of pleasantries that had suddenly been destroyed by the one worded question. The explicit way that Dan's mother looked down and his father awkwardly shifted in his chair made Dan bite the bottom of his lips till the crease in it issued forth blood, a degree of pain that Dan could barely feel in comparison to the harsh reality that his parents thought him to be a full blown nut job.

"Calmer. It helps keep him aware of everything that's going on around him in a very practical, stable manner."

"Are you saying he has no grip on reality?" The insulting tone of his mother's question made Dan stiffen up.      It was as if he were not really here, but an empty shell of a body that his parents were trying to pass off as their son, but really they were just speaking to Doctor Fuller. Dan had become a deaf mute, unable to hear exactly the intonation of his parents' words, and unable to speak in contradiction. His mother caught wind of the way that Dan sat up straight, his eyes focusing back out of the window. "Dan?" It had been the first time that his parents were inquiring him for the answer, instead of the man who had the diplomas hanging in his office to prove that he knew the answers. Dan glanced back over at his parents; the only two people who he had been under the assumption knew everything about him. But they stared at him as if he were a foster child suddenly being thrown into their care, and this was the first time they were setting eyes on him.

"What exactly is reality?"

"Dan," his mother's voice suddenly became stern, the predictable frustration towards Dan's impertinence growing. "That's a ridiculously unnecessary question."

"Is it?" He was standing in front of the window, looking at nothing in particular. As the silent moments droned on, he realized that he wasn't looking at anything at all. A shout came from the hallway, the clear image of a patient fighting to go back to his room, as the stomping of nurses revealed that exactly the opposite of the patient's wishes were going to happen. Dan's parents both looked towards the door, the unappetizing scenario igniting both of their imaginations.

"How much longer does he need to stay here Dr. Fuller?"

"Depends. He could behave rationally and be out in a week or he could continue to fight against the people who are trying to help him and it could be much longer." Dan still kept his back turned to the three others in the room, the stale air only mingling with the rising tempers that were ready to flare outwards like a fire.

"Dan, let them help you." His mother's plea struck a chord in him. It was a plea that any mother would give, wanting only the best for their child. But it was a plea that at that second Dan felt he couldn't fulfill, no matter the circumstances and no matter how much assistance he was given. His eyes wide and his face frozen in the constant look of coldness stayed planted on the window. His mother stood up, practically leaping for the door.

"I can't stay here. I'll be in the car."

"Mrs. Braddock—"

"Thank you for letting us come visit Dan, Dr. Fuller. Call if there's anything we need to know." A twitch cranked Dan's neck to one side, and from the corner of his eye he watched his mother take one more look at him, before disappearing through the door. A wave of abandonment gripped Dan. He turned back around, his forehead wrinkled as he took a deep breath to take it all in.

"I think I'm going to go back to my room, Doc." He ushered himself past his father, who stood up trying to catch his son, but his fingers only caught air as Dan slammed the door behind him and ran down the hall.

He sat on the edge of his bed, the sheets creasing from underneath his body. His vacant expression hadn't changed for minutes as he waited and listened for his father to exit the building, but the door across the hall still hadn't opened. His lips were cracked from where he bite down on them in his concentration, and his brow still was crinkled from the expression of thought that hadn't left his face. A rap on the door and suddenly his father entered. Dan watched his father's feet, his shoes reaching closer as they came over next to him. The bed sank as his father sat down, sagging sadly under the weight. His father held his hand over his mouth, his lips pursed in aggravation.

"I didn't mean to hurt Mom." It was all that Dan could muster to say, and it came from a cracked voice that was practically inaudible. It was a broken voice that he spoke with. His father nodded, keeping his hand firmly in front of his mouth, keeping his expression discreet.

"No one wants to see their kid in the hospital, Dan. That's just a fact of life. It's your mother's way of dealing with it I'm afraid." The two finally faced each other, the son chewing incessantly on his bottom lip, the father cupping his hands within one another, his fingers sweating profusely. The look between them though signified the new relationship that was now rooted between them. The past didn't matter now.

"Do you think I'm crazy?" His voice was little; his body hunched over like a limp rag doll. His father was surprised by the question, and for once, as a parent, he suddenly felt a huge pressure weigh down on him. Either answer that he could give to Dan would ultimately change everything between them. And yet not responding at all would break his son down, tearing him to pieces.

"Look, Dan. I don't know what you did to get yourself here—"

"It wasn't anything I did." Dan was wildly defensive, a shout exploding from him. His father watched his son fight back tears, and for minutes almost refusing to blink. Dan couldn't blink, he didn't want too. Every time he blinked, the color that flashed in his mind made him cringe.

"Well, whatever happened, it's over and done with now. It shouldn't matter anymore, right?" His father wanted to do something, give Dan any sign of comfort. But he couldn't force himself to place a reassuring hand on his son's shoulder. There wasn't even the possibility of hugging him. The disconnection between them right now was a huge weight bearing down on them, like a broken circuit that kept clicking for attention.

"You get the help you need Dan. That's all that your mom and I can ask for you to do. Everything will be in its right place." The last sentence made everything seem so broken, so disjointed and out of sync. Even this conversation between them seemed feigned, like an out of body experience for them both. His father paused, and then mumbled a goodbye. Dan could faintly feel his father's hand hover over his back, but it never lay to rest. The door clicked shut and then it was over. His parents had visited, they saw him, and they left. Dan lay down in his bed, wanting nothing more than to disappear completely.

"How do you think the visit with your parents went?"

(Pause)

"Dan?"

"What?"

"I asked you how you thought the visit with your parents went."

"That was over a week ago."

"I know. I specifically wanted to wait a while before asking."

"How thoughtful."

"And?"

(Pause)

"It was fine."

"Fine?"

"Well it wasn't full of happiness and sunshine if that's what you mean."

"Dan, we can have an honest conversation about this."

(Pause)

"It's just…no matter what I say, they'll never understand any of this."

"They can try though, and your parents care and love you. It is beyond evident that they will try to understand Dan."

"It doesn't matter."

"You don't think it will help you move on."

"No, it won't."

(Pause)

"Have you thought about going back to school at all?"

"What?"

"Are you listening to me at all today?"

"Yes, but you're asking very blunt questions. Let the mind process."

(Pause)

"Any answer would be nice Dan."

"Why would I think of school when I'm here?"

(Pause)

"What if I told you that I was planning on releasing you?"

(Pause)

"What is this, my Christmas gift? Nice joke Doc. It's everything I've always wanted."

"I'm being serious Dan."

(Pause)

"Why?"

"Why am I being serious?"

"No, why are you releasing me?"

"Because you don't need to be here. We've established this idea every week Dan."

"So?"

"Well, are you saying that you want to be here?"

"No."

"Then why are you so upset to hear that I'm releasing you? Do you think you shouldn't be released?"

"I…don't know. No, I guess."

"Good answer."

"What if I had answered yes you would have kept me here."

"Absolutely. Want to reevaluate what you said?"

"No."

"I'm releasing you Dan because I think that you have the ability to cope. You've been getting better with dealing with what happened every single week. You hardly talk about it anymore, you don't talk about Jamie anymore either."

"That's because I don't see Jamie."

"That's good."

(Pause)

"You're serious Doc?"

"Yes. Of course, I still think that it would be prudent and very necessary for you to have weekly visits. But I don't think it would be impractical to think that you couldn't start school again and move back into your apartment. If we're still in contact Dan, and you stick to your medications, I feel that you can go back to your life in a very healthy manner."

(Pause)

"You're not going to kick me out today, are you?"

"No, but I will be in contact with your parents in hopes that you can be released this weekend."

"Thanks."

"You're a part of this just as much as I am Dan."

"I know."

"Glad to hear that you agree with this."

"Yeah."

(Pause)

"Doc?"

"Yes Dan?"

"Do you think the cops have figured everything out?"

"Yes I do, Dan. Of course, there hasn't been any worthwhile news that answers either yes or no. If you're really concerned, why don't you contact them?"

"Nice joke Doc."

"I'm not joking Dan."

"Then I'd have to tell them what I saw."

"And what's the problem with that?"

(Pause)

"This question isn't changing your mind about releasing me, is it?"

"Not unless you want it to Dan."

"Good. But I'm still not going to them."

"It's hard to base a life off assumptions Dan. Wouldn't you just want the concrete answer that they have done everything they need to, and that you'll be safe?"

"Nothing's ever concrete Doc."

# XVII

The world seemed to have steadied; slowed back down to a pace that Dan felt he could keep up with. In essence, nothing at all had changed, but Dan banished that thought from his mind. The wobbly imbalance that had occurred over the past few months, as if he were constantly trying to configure his body on a balance beam had dwindled and Dan felt that he was finally steered towards a straight line again. Aiming for nothing, but nevertheless still aiming for something other than the chaos that had been stirring. There was an unmistakable digression, the clear fall back into a world that wasn't malleable. Dan was the elastic cord within the inflexible and unbroken world. He could, as Fuller had advised, either become a victim to his memories, or allow his consciousness to overcome it. What put a degree of elation in Dan's mind was his new acute awareness of the cynical life around him. It was depressing, dark, and left him as a useless figure that flitted form one spot to the next. But even still, he was suddenly in a world that he fully understood. He wasn't necessarily thriving, but he knew that he could muster on for some time before the cynicism would take over.

His parents had eagerly and graciously welcomed him back with open arms. His mother continued to hold the impression that if she blinked or looked away for even a second, Dan would disappear again. It therefore put forth onto Dan the challenge of having any minute alone to himself while back at home, his mother's ever-caring eye always on him. There was barely any conversation, but it was the serene silence that his mother clung to. If nothing was being said, then nothing awful was happening either. The world had fallen so effortlessly back into place again, a scattered, disjointed trail finally meeting with the original track. And Dan seemed to fall perfectly back into place; a shattered window whose pieces had gathered and collected again, resealed and solidified to its original form. He was quiet but self-assured. His parents took this as the miraculous cure.

The only one who had figured out that it was all a rouse was Emily. Upon Dan's return, she ran to him in a huge embrace, her smile lighting up the entire room. But in the few days that Dan decided to stay at the house, she suddenly become more distant and cold. She made it her mission to find out what really was happening, an unceasing giddiness in her ease to relentlessly sleuth and ask question after question.

At first Dan could ignore it, sleep it off, and close the door with a breathy evasiveness. But she became more fervent in her efforts. And in the time span of just a few days, Dan found himself stranded with his sister more than anyone else, even the ever-constant feel of his mother had disappeared. Emily was like an annoying insect that kept festering under Dan's skin. The only comforting fact that Dan has was knowing that even though she was undying in her efforts, it was the effort that made Dan increasingly more aware that she truly cared. She wasn't acting like the parents who wanted to live by the book, listing their family as perfect on paper, or the friend who pretended to know exceedingly more than she did about Dan's life. Emily was totally concerned, ready to divulge into the nitty-gritty details if it meant helping her brother.

"So what was the hospital like?"

"It was fine." The scene was already developing and playing out as Dan picked Emily up from school. He could already sense her anxious behavior as he equally shared the same feeling while he tapped the steering wheel.

"You know Mom and Dad lied to me at first? They told me you went back to school." Emily refused to move her eager wide eyes from Dan's face.

"They were just doing that to protect you." A laugh blurted

out from Emily's mouth.

"I knew it was a lie!"

"How?"

"You stopped calling to say hi." Dan felt an instant pang of guilt.

"Sorry Emily." She nodded, but stayed silent as she played with the zipper on her jacket. A simple distraction, but Dan could still see in the line of distress marked in her forehead.

"Hey, I'm okay you know." Dan tried beyond belief to drop the subject. Emily just looked at him with eyes that showed a girl who was well beyond her years.

"Then why did you have to go at all?" She had stopped toying with her jacket, looking back up directly at him. No response. "Dan come on, we used to tell each other everything."

"Not this time Emily."

"I won't tell Mom and Dad."

"It's not about that Emily." She could see his jaw clench, his teeth gritting together as his frustration built up. She only had a few more words to convince him, or the jig was up.

"Dan, I don't think you're crazy or anything. I just want to know."

"Well I'm not going to tell you everything anymore!" The words stung. Instantly, like a thorn being pricked sharply into the skin. The car ride continued on silently, Dan's eyes on the road while Emily had averted her stare to out the window, staring at the line of trees that whizzed past.

"Emily—"

"You hate this don't you? All of this."

"No I don't."

"Just admit it Dan."

"Emily," he firmly said her name, making his sister finally look back over at him, but not before quickly swiping a tear off her cheek. "I don't hate this. I don't hate you if that's what you think. I..."

"Why can't everything just be normal?" The question hung in the air without an answer.

By the end of a week, Dan had become determined to slowly show signs that he was ready to go back to school, though his mother especially showed no response as to climbing back into the car and making the trek to the campus that she'd have to leave her son at. She had just gotten him back, and she didn't want him to leave as soon as he wanted to, it was plain and simple. But she silently acknowledged the packed up suitcase, the backpack refilled with books, and the growing abundance of wrapped up electric cords. Dan and his parents finally exchanged the few short sentences, and decided on the day to leave for school.

But it had arrived, and all four of them seemed to walk on edge. Emily had clamped up completely, sitting in her room at the edge of her bed, waiting nervously for Dan to walk out the door, wanting to say a few last minute things and still relaying the fight in the car over and over in her mind. Their mother was scurrying around as if this were the first time Dan had ever left the house, rechecking for things that he could take back with him. Their father stayed out of sight, flipping through channels in the living room till his wife and son finally took the plunge to walk out the door.

Like Emily, Dan kept replaying the words that he had said to her a few days earlier. It was the coldest they had probably ever been to each other, and the whole entire conversation played on an endless loop inside his head. He resisted with every fiber in his being, unwilling to give Emily the satisfaction and the answers that she wanted, and reluctant to fall into the dream-like reality that so many people weakly clung to. Because the truth that remained was that though he could stick himself into the illusion of a normal life, Dan knew that it was the most improbably goal that he could hold on to. It was the solidifying moment, in which Dan realized that his sister was much more aware of the same world than he thought, that he realized how much she had made herself grow up for him since he was gone. It was the astounding factor of how one significant event could change one so much.

Dan was standing in the kitchen, alone, when Emily finally emerged from downstairs. Their father was starting the car and their mother was packing it up with the last of Dan's things, both completely out of sight. Emily suddenly situated the center island of the kitchen between her and her older brother. All that stood between them was the inanimate object, but she had the advantage of placing herself perfectly in the doorway outside. It was just as strong of a barrier that it became an immense fortress. Her eyes belied the disappointment that she tried to hide.

"Just talk to me Dan," she pleaded. He sighed, shaking his head. "You're not the same!"

"I'm standing right here!" Dan bellowed, his mind tried from the constant fighting that had occurred between the two in just the minimal set of hours that he had been home. They had never raised their voices so much till now, and the strain that both felt sapped away the energy between them. "I'm still me."

"No you're not." And there it was. The simple statement that even if he tried desperately to revert back to his old life, it wasn't even in the realm of possibilities for succeeding. It was the first time Emily had described any doubt to Dan. The shocked look on her face was due to the surprising fury that had suddenly risen in her, a temper that before this moment she had never wanted to behold. She ran from the room immediately without saying another word, leaving Dan dumbfounded, his hands gripping the counter, his fingers a bloodless white.

The apartment had remained unchanged, with perhaps the only exception being the isolated corner where Dan's room was placed. The room was still dark, shades drawn and dust settling on the various areas that Dan hadn't touched in ages, and would proceed not to touch even now that he was back. The books still laid stacked on the desk, the dresser filled with miscellaneous little piles of objects and coins that had accumulated in his bag and pockets over the course of last semester.

Dan's mom instantly raised the shades of the room, emitted forth the natural light. The room looked drastically different when the rays of light touched every corner. It didn't lit up as Dan though it would, but created more shadows that he had been completely unaware of. He set down the suitcase and backpack on his bed, and then the room's furnishings were complete. His parents didn't linger as much as he assumed they would, but rather helped carry everything into his apartment and then delivered a short goodbye. And then they left just as quickly as they came; acting like this was the most natural and prudent thing to do.

It was as if the past month hadn't even happened. Dan shuffled around his room, refusing to unpack anything just yet, but also not moving anything either. Everything was a reminder of the last night that he was here. And though he didn't want the memento that everything wasn't a dream, he still felt that it wasn't right to dishevel everything in the room just for the sake of change.

"Hey, you're back." His roommate stood at the door, but just clear of the actual spaced that marked Dan's room. It was as if he needed a special incantation to enter the room, which he looked dubiously into as if it were cursed, more terrifying than it actually was. "We were wondering what happened, you left so quickly finals week."

"Yeah…" Dan shuffled on his feet. His roommate just as stiffly tapped his hand against the banister of the door.

"Everything okay man?"

"Yeah, it's fine." It was the unspoken rule that Dan had with his roommates. Even with how long they had known each other and lived with each other, the code of silence was never broken. If one of them didn't wish to talk about it, the subject was most likely never brought up again, even if it held a severe seriousness. And this was how they moved on, spending the rest of the night drinking the occasionally beers, ordering disgusting food, and settling on the couch for hours of useless television and entertaining discussions. Dan hardly spoke about the break, but no one cared, it was a finished topic. The point was that Dan was back; clearly acting normal, and they had a few more days of rowdy carelessness before diving back into a new semester.

Dan thrived in the exceedingly relaxed night, the lavishing nothingness that brought him back into a world that he craved. He sat without thought to the medications that sat near his bedside, or the cold hospital that he had just spent close to a month in. It was a blurred nightmare that Dan was hardly concerned of anymore, a memory that one assumes will never be forgotten, but they realize that they can't even remember that faintest details of it. Faces are suddenly hazy, when before they were striking. Conversations that once could be recited over and over like an ongoing monologue were now just distant hushes and whispers. It was wholly comforting, knowing that one day perhaps this whole year could just be a remote number of complete unimportance.

The hours of the night passed on, and it was severely late when Dan sauntered back into his room. Closing the door, he laid down on his bed, taking a deep sigh of cold air that refueled his lungs. But the darkness waned on, and the silence of the night allowed for thoughts to creep into his mind. Dan stared up at the ceiling, with his eyes every once in a while glancing at his phone, which continued to lay lifeless as the hours continued to tick away. But there was no call, no need for him. He could be invisible and obsolete once again. Dan wasn't scared by this revelation at all.

"So, you're back at school."

"Yep."

"What classes are you taking?"

"Wow, we're back to the small talk. Alright, I'm taking a couple psych courses, a history and English class that I need to get out of the way."

"Are you happy with this?"

"Gotta graduate, don't I?"

"So the idea of school and graduating isn't a bad idea for you anymore?"

(Pause)

"It is what it is, I guess. I mean it's not terrifying. What else am I going to do, you know?"

"I see."

(Pause)

"What were you doing before classes started?"

"Do you want a play by play Doc?"

"Just a simple answer will suffice Dan."

"I hung with my roommates, friends. Kinda chilled for a bit I guess. It was nice."

"Good."

(Pause)

"So are we going to get to the real discussion Doc?"

"Are you still taking your medications?"

"Yes."

"Good. You're not having trouble with them anymore."

"They make me feel fine, isn't that what they're supposed to do?"

"Yes, of course."

"Then they're doing their job."

(Silence)

"Have you seen Jamie?"

(Pause)

"I thought we weren't going to bring her up anymore Doc?"

"We don't have to talk about her if you don't want to. I was just curious."

(Pause)

"No, I haven't."

"Does this upset you?"

(Silence)

"Dan?"

(Silence)

"Why does this upset you?"

"How do you know it upsets me?"

"Judging from your silence—"

"Maybe I just don't care anymore so there's no reason to talk about her."

"Is that the case Dan?"

(Silence)

"Dan?"

"No."

"Why does it upset you Dan?"

"I...I don't know. I think of her, and all I think about is the past few months, and then it all comes back to me. And I don't want to think about any of that anymore. But if I think of Jamie I can't help it! But when I don't think about her..."

"Yes?"

"I mean, logically, she kind of helped me get through that, in a way."

"Did she though? If thinking about her now only reminds you of all the bad things that happened, how is she helping?"

(Pause)

"I don't know...she just did. I liked talking to her."

"There are plenty of other people you can talk to. Plenty of people who might be a better influence."

"I needed her."

"What?"

"I needed her. I don't know how else to say it. With everything that happened last semester, the only thing that pushed me through it was her."

"That's not how I see it Dan."

"Well it doesn't matter how you see it, does it?"

"Don't get angry Dan!"

"Well then stop making her seem like the bad guy!"

(Silence)

"I understand what you have against her Doc, but that doesn't mean I have to think that way too."

"I think you should."

(Silence)

"Let's just drop it. I'm not seeing her anyways, so why should we keep talking about her."

"Consider the matter dropped. How was it visiting your family before you went back to school?"

"Fine."

"Really?"

(Pause)

"Of course not."

"Why not?"

"My parents act as if I wasn't even admitted to that hospital, pretending as if nothing is wrong. And my sister practically hates me now."

"Well, it's hard for them to understand when they don't know what happened Dan."

"Well that's not going to make me tell them."

"I understand that Dan, but you must understand why they are acting the way that they are then. Without the proper information, your family can't understand the reasoning behind what you did."

"I know…"

"Do you still refuse to walk past that alley?"

(Silence)

"Dan?"

(Silence, tape finishes)

# XVIII

Dan stood in front of the open window, watching the sun peak over the buildings, though the sky still held a gray bleakness. His fingers traced the cool windowpane, and for a second a mist encircled his fingers, the window melting underneath his touch. Once removed, his fingers remained as white as frosted glass. The window returned to its icy state. Dan stood, but thought nothing. His mind was frantic, but his body held a sluggish weight that mocked his ever-wandering mind. The clock ticked, signaling the passing of only a single minute, though it felt so much more drawn out. He finally moved, a quaking step. A bottle that had once contained pills lay empty, abandoned on its side. Dan took no notice.

It was with an astounding amount of incredible ease that Dan participated in the life of a college student once again. He without second thought walked into his first classes. He opened his notebook, ink filling the blank lines with etched black markings. He was severely concentrated, yet on edge. Everything was repetitive, but did not perturb him. The soothing feeling of being able to simply walk from one room to the next without worry deconstructed any negative thought he could possible possess. He could stay completely focused on what his professors were lecturing on, but yet his mind still had the freedom to wander. It was with grave reluctance that he first fell into a cloud of thought, but felt no tug of anxiety. It was a necessity, this constant thought processing. His mind and body refused to be knocked from this rhythm. And nothing in the world seemed strong enough to stop him.

It was a curious thing, to watch a switch be so easily clicked in Dan's mind, alternating so fast from one thought to the next. Dan couldn't be shaken from this state. Nothing in front of him was a certainty, and yet it was still all predetermined. He was watching the ink of his pen, spreading along the stark, pristine white paper in detail, when the assembly of students suddenly rose, processing out of the classroom. In the wake of the group was Dr. Arnstein, collecting papers at his desk with archetypical academic persona. He looked up to see the individual student who had yet to leave.

"Mr. Braddock, good to see you back." The pen stopped, the ink welling up into a dark circle. Dan quickly shut the notebook, capping the pen and tossing it into his bag. Arnstein had lost the look of foreboding that he had frequently placed on Dan, a gentle composure settling in his face.

"Good to be back."

"And how are things?"

"Fine." The curtness couldn't be ignored by either party, each wishing to play the part. As a teacher, Arnstein felt compelled to help, but found himself holding back. Perhaps it was the cowardly fear of falling into a plot he wanted nothing of. Or perhaps his kindness towards his students was really always the fabrication he willed it not to be. For Dan, he simply had nothing to say. He had already dug the hole deep enough that if he fell in there was no way of getting out. And he had finally managed to claw his way back up to the surface ground. Why spoil it now?

Arnstein moved back towards his desk, giving himself amble distance as he separated Dan from himself with the large piece of furniture. Grabbing his belongings, he gave a friendly smile to Dan, but in his eyes was something akin to sadness, even disappointment. It was sent towards Dan for a split second, perhaps even missable if Dan hadn't been careful enough. And then Arnstein disappeared, slipping around the corner.

For Dan to have concerned himself on the look, dawdling on it for even a moment was to inch back to the end of that pit he had so pointedly avoided. He brushed it away as if it were a buzzing fly.

The student owed no explanation to the professor, just as the professor couldn't truly expect a personal and approachable relationship to be established fully. The image of a consoling relationship was never what Dan had anticipated, yet it annoyed him that he dwelled on the look Arnstein gave him. Why disappointment? Dan had never given cause to justify that particular feeling. *Just let it go.* But he couldn't, it was gnawing at him fervently, like a scratch it couldn't contain. The phone in his pocket suddenly buzzed to life, dragging Dan away from his perplexed dilemma that ate away at him.

"Yeah?"

"Dude, do you have a class right now?" The ability for a person's tone to change a benign question was extraordinary. Dan felt himself freeze in the doorway, his fingers wrapped tightly around the aged wood. His eyes roamed the halls, scouring the isolated area, but no one was there save for the passing student sprinting late to her next class.

"Dan?"

"No, I don't. Why?"

"You should come back to the apartment."

The concrete sidewalk slammed along the bottoms of Dan's feet, forcing him forward with every step. His apartment, being situated in a spot that realistically created not too long of a walk to campus suddenly seemed like a marathon that had no conceivable end. Dan felt himself growing more and more troubled as he walked on. The notion that he could stop, turn away and ignore the call seemed like only a far off possibility, too far from his reach. *Who the hell ends a conversation like that?* No details, no warning of what Dan could be walking into. He turned the corner to his street. His eyes fixed themselves on his feet for the first few residences, the damned site suddenly rearing its ugly monstrous head and leering at Dan. A flash of color made his head snap up. Two cop cars had themselves perfectly centered in front of his apartment, a set up obstacle course for Dan to traverse through. The apartment zoomed towards him. It was rapidly too close for comfort. Dan spun around. A whirling sound that mimicked a thousand radios screaming white noise playing his head. A head was the unmentionable place. Behind him were the spinning lights. He was a misbehaved child who had gotten trapped between two parents. No matter which way he ran, it was right into the open arms of a retaliator, forced to punish him. He was only left with the decision of which parent was easiest to deal with. He picked the apartment, ascending the steps with feet filled with lead.

*It's nothing serious…it's nothing.* The repetition of the phrase did nothing to ease Dan as he slowly climbed the countless steps to his door. He paused in front of it, staring into the grooves of the wood as if they contained some clue as to what he was about to face. He placed his hand carefully on it and pushed. The door swung open, gliding smoothly on its hinges. With a rush of air behind him, Dan was beckoned in. His roommate who had called stood dumbfounded, his eyes wildly searching the room for anything that could deeply incriminate him. Two police officers stood, both tall and both with faces turned towards Dan. He recognized neither face. One was straight blond hair, but a reasonable face. He offered nothing but a look of cooperation. The other had dark hair, and equally dark eyes. They roamed every object as if something was mysterious about the apartment, though in hindsight it was only a poorly cared for accommodation for starving college students. The look he gave Dan was condescending. Dan instantly knew that he would have to put up a fight to keep up with this cop.

"Are you Dan?" the dark haired cop spoke up first, his voice dripping with a haughty air, taking his authority way too literally. Did Dan dare answer? He momentarily thought of creating a whole new name for himself. A new identity so that he could exclaim with embarrassment that he was only a friend and leave his roommate high and dry without another trace.

"Yeah, Dan Braddock," he found himself answering.

"There was a break in to the building. A couple doors were

found open, including yours. Now your roommate said nothing looks taken, but do you mind checking your room as well?" Dan glanced at his roommate, who's freaked expression had subsided quite a bit. Sadly, Dan was pretty positive his had not. He knew he wasn't in trouble, but the way the dark haired cop looked at him made his insides crawl nervously. He stiffly sidestepped past the cops, refusing to meet their eyes. *What if they know me?*

"It's probably nothing to worry about. We'll check to see if anything was taken, report it. Regardless, a cop will patrol the area, but the person who tried to break in isn't likely to do it again."

Dan walked into his room. Dark haired cop was close on his heels, sneaking up like a predator. Dan could have scanned his room a thousand times and known that nothing was missing. But now the room looked foreign, as if he had never walked into it before. It was as if another person this whole year had lived here, and he was only a spectator examining the life of a young man. His eyes swept over everything, taking in every item and stashing it away like a photo into his memory. Everything was in the details, and right now it was the details that counted. Dan circled the room and a panic settled in when he finally noticed dark haired cop, standing in the doorway with his bulky arms crossed over his chest, leaning against the doorway with a smug air lingering around him. He gave a calm and collected expression towards Dan, though it was feigned with every crack that appeared around his tight lips that had turned upwards. The cop's eyes were roaming, searching for messages hidden with the details. Dan felt his chest heaving, his breath a thick wave that engulfed his lungs, but brought no relief.

A direct line from the cop's eyes to the object he was looking at and the orange pharmaceutical bottle suddenly entered the scene. The label was clearly legible, Dan's information a huge billboard for anyone to read. *Did they read it, the men who were here?* Dan's eyes, like a mirror, rose up at seemingly the same time as the cop's. The cop's face belied no true feelings, holding the same nonchalant look, as if this whole excursion was a waste of his time. Dan's eyes were glassy with panic, his hand twitching as he tried to decipher whether the better decision would be to pick the bottle up, or leave it behind in its discarded place.

"There doesn't look like anything's missing," Dan remarked with feigned coolness in his voice. His fingers, damp with sweat, traced the rim of the empty bottle, which tipped as it was spun around, tilting like a ballerina dancing in a circle. *Why this? Of all the things to leave out in the open, why this?* That particular item was the only reminder that Dan left to himself, a reminder that everything before had happened.

"Nothing?" Dark haired cop's questioning look seemed like a dead giveaway to Dan. His face had the same stoic look, the edges of his mouth pursed in contemplation. But his eyes, those piercing dark eyes that centered on Dan held the vague notion of something askew, a hidden secret. Dan's fingers wrapped around the bottle, and the cop watched every single precise motion as Dan picked it up, tucking it into the sleeve of his shirt, his hand cupped around it. Dan tried to swallow, but the taste of bile was still reminiscent.

"No, everything looks just the way I left it this morning." This wasn't Dan's voice. It couldn't be, for deep down inside Dan was shuddering, but the voice answered with such smoothness that Dan knew it couldn't be real. The two held their ground, standing facing each other with only a few feet between them. It was enough space that Dan felt safe enough from the cop. But it was still enough space that the cop could move quickly if need be. The electricity between them dramatically faded as the cop tapped his hand on the doorway, his face still tight lipped in decision.

"Fair enough."

He walked through the hall, his sharp shoes reseeding away from Dan. The bottle emerged from Dan's sleeve, a cold lifeless item in his hand. He held it out in front of him, as if it were a threatening creature that would bite him. Muffled voices came forth from the hall, a calm conversation between the three men. Dan closed his eyes, his heart still thumping and his breath still ragged. His fingers around the bottle were still shaking, the sweat still gathering around the sleek edge of the bottle. *It's nothing!* He screamed at himself. The bottle slipped from his hand, flopping down into a pile of clothes. Dan stalked down the hall, his face determined to hold the stony expression. The ability for the cops to stand squarely facing the young men till they squirmed was appalling, and yet they took advantage of this power as Dan reentered the kitchen.

"So, we'll definitely put in a report, and have officers patrol the area for a while," it was the second cop that held the polite persona, while dark haired cop was looking precariously around the room still. Both Dan and his roommate awkwardly stood without saying a word, looking down as if they were the ones accused.

"Call us if you see anything else wrong." Dan's roommate nodded as the cop continued to usher out precautions, steady words of advice. However, Dan's eyes were glued on the other uniformed man, his glare intensifying with each passing second that the cops remained in the apartment. His roommate was too dimwitted to notice. The Dark haired cop was ignoring Dan's antagonizing attempts to meet his stare, and suddenly fell onto a perfectly square piece of paper with scribbled writing that was stuck to the fridge. *Son of a bitch,* Dan thought frantically.

"Thank you, we'll let you know if anything else happens," Dan's roommate watched as Dan backed a step while the other cop took a step closer to the note, carefully reading the number.

"Did you ever call?" Dark haired cop interrupted his partner's attempted farewell. Dan's roommate gargled a noise and turned to Dan for the answer. Dan rubbed his hands nervously together.

"Um, yeah it was for a parking citation last semester," he said quietly, licking his lips fervently. The cop nodded, still staring at the numbers as if a coded message would suddenly appear in between the numbers.

"Good."

"Just be careful when walking home. The crime rate in this area has definitely risen in the past couple of months," the second cop tried to take the conversation back to the present, tucking the notepad in his hand back into his pocket. Dan's roommate shuffled on his feet.

"Yeah, kind of like that murder back in the fall."

Dan's heart stopped. It wasn't the thought that his heart had stopped; it was unsettling feeling that he actually felt a flutter as his heart skipped. He couldn't feel a beat in his chest but the pounding in his head could have been strong enough to split his skull. Blotches, sports appeared in his eyesight, blurring the whole entire scene in front of him. He couldn't catch his breath.

"That was crazy," his roommate kept rambling as if the topic were helping the situation, talking like an ignorant imbecile, but both the cops had noticed Dan. It was a rush, but not the kind that flowed adrenaline throughout Dan's body. Rather, it was a stifled, growing force that wanted to erupt through him, tearing him at the seams.

"How do you know about that?" Dan whispered. But it wasn't the question that made everyone in the room focus on Dan, it was the way in which he wanted only his roommate to hear what he had to say, the words almost inaudible. His roommate turned to him with a baffled expression. The cops seemed to be closing in, seeping closer towards Dan.

"What do you mean man? It was all over the news. Wasn't that how you heard about it?" Dan couldn't speak, and all three of the others in the room were now waiting for a conformation. The air was stifling but he couldn't leave. There was no way out, he was trapped completely. An intolerable discomfort settled in the air, and it took all of Dan's will power not to break down in front of the three standing in front of him.

"Yeah...yeah definitely...read it..." It wasn't even a full sentence. That alone showed how much Dan wasn't capable of doing at the moment. He had faltered with those five words alone, croaking them out of his mouth as if he were choking. All three still stared at him quizzically. Dan disturbingly rubbed the top of his hand until dark haired cop's stare made him freeze, dropping his hand limply to his side but quaking as if found the absence of any motion at all to be more agonizing than scratching the layers of skin from the top of his hand.

"Hey, did you ever catch the guys who killed her?" Dan stared in amazement at the absurdity of hearing his roommate's question. The dark haired cop clenched his jaw, glancing at Dan who felt he was sweating profusely. It had to be clearly visible at this point. The other cop calmly diffused the growing uneasiness within the room.

"That information really shouldn't be disclosed."

"Well, are we safe?"

"Of course, by all means. As long as you're smart about what you do. The victim was out late that night, completely alone and vulnerable." The excuse that the cop released infuriated Dan with seconds.

"Don't blame that on the girl. It's not her fault she was murdered!" Dan shouted. The immediate wave of mortification that immersed the room made Dan want to take back every word he just said. Both cops were now looking sternly at Dan. His roommate simply stood with his mouth open in shock by Dan's outburst.

"No blame is being placed on her, only the advice to take precaution. I meant no offense. Did you know her?" The gleam in the dark haired cop's eye was a warning to Dan. *Shit, he knows. He fucking knows. They don't have the killers. They must have found the killers, it would have been announced if they hadn't. Would it though? Is known panic better off than blissful ignorance to two murderers still walking in the open? They're still out there. The bottle! Oh god...*

The string of thoughts made Dan completely unresponsive. The cops said more to him, but their words were only murmurs that Dan barely paid attention to. He didn't respond to anything else they said. The rest of the blurred scene consisted of the cops respectfully leaving, though not before each authoritative figure gave Dan one last apprehensive look, a dubious frown of doubt.

The infallible anxiety that gripped Dan couldn't be shattered.

It was an immense figure that drew closer and closer till Dan felt the ground beneath him crumble, and his body fall back into the miserable pit that he had dug for himself. He could feel his grip, his center. Just barely, like sand slipping through his fingers. He was unable to do anything about it or pick it up. It was just blowing in the wind now. To try and gather back every grain of sand was impossible. It was easier for him to slip into the insanity.

# XIX

His roommate sat there. He was perpetually staring, looking, contemplating, and even breathing in Dan's direction. He was like an animal, frozen in space and yet continuously using every one of his senses to better understand what his next move should be. He would glance up and then quickly revert his eyes away. If his roommate was the animal, shrunk and cornered, then Dan was the larger beast, waiting patiently for his roommate to crack. But in the meantime, the way that his roommate's eyes constantly glanced at every one of his twitches, analyzed every sigh, made Dan on the brink of losing his mind. All Dan wanted to do was heave up every last drop of himself.

They both stood, facing each other as if standing off and preparing for a dual. A drop of water was dislodged from the faucet in the kitchen. The whirl of electricity coursed through the dim light above them. The silence was dangerously palpable. Dan knew that the next words he dares to speak would be essential in maintaining any sort of friendship with the person standing across from him. One wrong word, one angled tone that was leaning towards anything that resembled insanity and he would be looking at an acquaintance that would look at him just as oddly as everyone else on the street did. His roommate was afraid of even staggering an inch, tripping forward and suddenly giving Dan space to pounce on him. He refused to repeat the incident just minutes ago with the cops. Gathering up courage, he said one pointed line towards Dan. It was blatant and sharp.

"What the hell was that?"

Dan walked to the sink. His roommate took a step back.

They both froze, staring at each other still. Dan reached for a glass from the cabinet, the sink still dripping with incredible effort, as if trying to surge forth and break the tension. Dan's fingers flicked the faucet on, and the glass filled up. His roommate was leaning against the kitchen table, his grips gripping the chair behind him. The glass rose to Dan's lips, but the only thing that either of the two boys could concentrate on was the shaking hand that held the glass, making the water within to swirl and sputter against the edge. Dan took a quick swig, quickly setting the glass harshly against the cheap counter. His fingers still shook, though they held onto the glass with all of their might, an icy white.

"It's nothing man," Dan replied simply. His back was turned to his roommate, for the doubt that was in his eyes, the same doubt that trapped in his body into a cycle of tiny convulsions, was clear on his whole face. His fingers slid down the glass as his roommate's voice broke the silence.

"That wasn't nothing. That was…that was freaky. You suddenly jumped on those guys!"

"Just let it go," Dan whispered, closing his eyes tightly and trying to ride the sweaty fever that suddenly coursed through his whole body.

"You're lucky you didn't get in trouble for freaking out on those cops. I've never seen you do that—"

"Just let it go." Dan's fingers inched back up the cup, fumbled across the lips of the glass.

"What?"

"Drop it, okay!" The fury that raked his body suddenly caused his fingers to clench around the lip of the glass, dragging the cup off the counter as he spun around. For a split second the glass hung in the air and then slammed against the tiled floor, shattering into a thousand pieces. Dan felt beads of sweat running down the sides of his face, soaking into his hair. His chest heaved, but his lungs couldn't catch any whiff of air. His roommate blinked, his jawbone shifting from side to side as he clenched his teeth. Dan was looking down, air whizzing through his nose as he tried to calm down. The water licked the edges of the glass, spreading serenely across the floor.

"Screw this." Dan didn't have to watch to know that his roommate fled to his room. He didn't need to listen to know that he was throwing items into a bag, zipping it up. And he didn't need to flinch when his roommate stalked back out quickly, opened the door without a second glance and then slammed the door behind him, leaving a ringing in Dan's ears.

All Dan proceeded to do was back himself into the living room, his knees brushing the couch before he collapsed into the furniture, which graciously accepted Dan with open arms. His eyes didn't waver from the spot on the ceiling, where a single crack ran along the plaster and paint. Just one more crack, but this one couldn't be fixed as easily as the others. Pick at it, and more bits would break off, a tiny heap that contained too much confusion to be put in order again.

*Dead leaves crunched under his feet. The living room of his apartment disappeared further and further away from him as he walked deeper into the woods. Patches of light from the moon caught on a few of the leaves and branches around him, but otherwise the night around him was black, leaving Dan blindly following a trail from what he could remember.*

*"Hey Doc."*

*A conversation played in his head, and he couldn't tell if it was real or part of the dream. Consciousness was never simple.*

*"Dan, what a pleasant surprise. I haven't seen you in a while. How are you?"*

*"I'm doing just fine."*

*A twig cracked into two, like the feeble bones of a decaying animal, and Dan continued on.*

*"You look well."*

*"Thanks. Guess that's what a month in this place will do to you."*

*"How's school?"*

*"Fine, I guess. Haven't really put my feet fully in the water you, you know?"*

*"Yeah."*

*A screech from overhead and the rustle of wings brushed close to Dan, sending a chill down his spine. Literally everything in front of him had morphed onto a deep black, only the faint edges of things appearing at the last second. But he continued to walk on.*

*"Do you still think about it?"*

*"Naw, there's no reason to anymore, right?"*

*"Right. Good for you Dan."*

*A patch of light was drawing closer. Dan knew that in an instant he would face the same thing he did every time he returned to this particular clearing. It was the dying deer. He pulled a thick branch towards him and stepped closer.*

*"Still talk to Jamie?"*

*The deer was gone and in its place was a body. Its skin was smooth, like alabaster. Only one part of it was broken. Where flesh should have been perfectly even, edges of it now rose into the air, leaving ugly craters within the body's once perfect skin. Dan shrunk back, but the body drew closer, as if the ground underneath suddenly was a conveyor belt that he had no control of, and no way of moving onto it to escape.*

*"Not really."*

*"Good."*

*A bump in the ground and the body flopped over like a sack of discarded objects. Its arms flayed wide open, exposing the chest with puncture wounds that were deep, jagged and raw. Blood pooled at the edges, thick and moist. Dan's pulse ran, wanting nothing more than to share this quickened pulse with the lifeless thing in front of him. It drew closer. Its neck turned. And her face stared at Dan. A silent scream came from Dan's mouth.*

*"I'll see you around Doc."*

Dan sprung off the couch. He rushed to the bathroom, flicking on the light but not even shutting the door before lifting the lid off the toilet and retching into it. His body in the curled fetal position around the toilet rocked back and forth, his chest heaving till it ached. The sickness stopped and Dan held his heavy head over the toilet. The conversation replayed over and over, an endless loop that was drowning out every other sound. And the body, her body, was all that Dan saw. He flushed the toilet, his hand wiping his lips. But he still remained huddled against the cold porcelain, the coolness rushing through his heated body.

*Did that happen?* The conversation, none of which was seen, was so real, vivid. It was like it had been directly played into Dan's ear from the tapes as he slept. *It couldn't have happened...*

A flash of light caught his attention and his eyes turned to his phone that lay on the floor. The phone read one missed call. Dan dialed for voicemail, the dull ring tone fading into his ear as he pressed the phone up to his ear. A crackle and a gasp started the message, and then for a few seconds there was only silence, with the quiet white noise of the world around the caller humming in the background.

"Dan?" It was Jamie's voice. Dan stood up, crossing towards the window with the intention of finding her standing right outside his apartment. But the street was empty, save for one car that was parked about two hundred feet away, directly in between two streetlights. Panic gripped Dan and he slowly closed the blinds, pressing the cheap plastic against the windowpane.

"Dan?" His attention was back on the message, his body still rigid and upright. "Dan…if you get this please call me back…" A choke and Jamie was rubbing her nose with the back of her hand. "Please?" It was a plea. "Please just…Dan…" The rambling voice of Jamie, the husky sharp intakes of breath was all that filled Dan's head. She paused, taking a deep breath. A shuffle of feet resounded out of the phone as she tripped, backing herself against the wall of a building.

"Look…" Her voice was a whisper, soft and shaky but still harsh. "I know I haven't been around a lot recently but…" Her voice drew even quieter, almost inaudible. So much so that Dan's fingers were ghostly white as he crushed his phone against his ear.

"I need your help." Sobs choked her words and suddenly she was running. For seconds, possibly minutes, all Dan heard was the pounding of footsteps as Jamie ran and ran. She was barely breathing but when she did it was mixed with tears and tiny screams.

"Dan!" she shrieked in hushed tone. "They're after me! Dan… they've been following me. I—"

*End of new messages.*

The phone dropped from Dan's hand, bouncing off the floor with a dull thud. *They're after me! Dan!* Her words were now shouts in his head, no longer the stifled sobs that had been impregnated into his phone for all eternity. Now it was all that he could hear. He dashed forward, his fingers splitting open the blinds. His eyes peeked through the black night. The car was still there. *Son of a bitch!* Dan slammed the blinds shut. He ducked down from the window, sinking further towards the ground. The same whirl from the light overhead could be heard. But it was gravely overshadowed as Dan heard the car's engine rev up, roaring to life like a demon. His body shook, his fingers that were wrapped around his legs trembling. He could feel the car inch closer to the apartment, driving past the building ever so surreptitiously. And then the tires screeched and the vehicle sped away. But it got what it came for. Dan slammed his head against the wall behind him. Tiny prickles of light flashed in his eyes as he squeezed them shut. He knew that his head was throbbing from hitting it so hard, but it was barely felt. *They know. They found Jamie…and they know. They know everything. Fuck.*

He rushed down the stairs, taking them two at a time. The apartment lay in the same condition as when his roommate had left. The wreckage of the glass still lay sprawled across the floor, the tiny shards sparkling in the dim light that glowed over them. His phone that had been carelessly dropped still lit up, an endless litany of the same benign woman voice asking relaying options on how to proceed with the most recent message. On the table were Dan's keys.

He pushed the door open and he his foot hit concrete. Like a brick wall he suddenly stopped as a whoosh of cold air came at him. He looked behind him to where the front door of the apartment building swung slowly shut on its hinges, the lock clicking into place. He paused, looked down at his feet, up to his legs and to where his arms hung. It was at this moment that Dan sat quizzically looking at the complexity of a human arm, and how strange it looked for a tiny wrist to morph into a flat hunk of flesh that spread out into his fingers. The fingers still shook uncontrollably, caked with layers of sweat now that Dan had taken no regard too. His mind was blank. All that it contained were the fitful cries of Jamie, the body from his dream and the feigned conversation. That conversation kept coming back to haunt him. It was everything that he wanted to happen, and it was just out of reach.

There was no one in the street, no sign of any life. There was only Dan and the streetlights that flickered on and off, leading him down the sidewalk like beacons toward his destination. Only one place stuck out in his mind, and that's where Dan's feet led him. His stomach still rolled with discomfort, his heart still rapidly thumping against his chest. His eyes were red, brimming with tears that Dan tried to muster forth, but couldn't come up with even the courage to cry. The occasional rustle made Dan stop, jump, turn and cower till he found the source of the sound. Tiny animals that basked in the same darkness of the night greeted Dan from underneath bushes, car tries and house corners, their eyes tiny yellow beads against the black surroundings. They emerged like Dan from their hiding spots, relinquishing the comfort of warmth and scampering out into the cold night.

Dan felt along his pockets at the items that he had grabbed, suddenly wishing that he had picked up his phone. He wanted to hear the message again. Maybe Jamie just spooked herself. Maybe there was already a second message, saying that everything was just fine and that there was nothing to worry about. Dan scoffed. The ability for his mind to play tricks and mock him was breathtaking, like sucking him into a dream where everything had been flipped upside down and was perfect again.

He turned the corner. The crossroad was here. Either he stays on the same side, where the spot was, or he cross and miss it completely. His feet naturally turned to cross. It was a ritual, one that he felt he could never break. But something in him stopped his feet from turning. His eyes were square on the shadowed area, the spot where it all happened. His feet kept forward, and he slowly made his way down the wrong side of the street. *Dan...they've been following me...* Dan kept walking, his feet starting to feel like lead as he got closer and closer. *Dan, they're after me!* The two building that shrouded the spot loomed over him as if they were the tallest buildings in the world. His hand reached into his pocket, his fingers sliding along the various items that he had tucked away. One was the flimsy wallet that he had carried around for years. He pulled it out his pocket, cradling it in his hand.

The alley. It was still here, though it was never going to disappear, no matter how many times Dan wished. Headlights suddenly appeared behind, illuminating the whole entire alleyway. Dan never realized how small the space actually was. Barely three people could fit in here. And yet that was all it took that night, just three people. Dan spun around when the headlights didn't fade, when the car didn't turn. The car stood at the end of the road that was directly in across from the alley. Dan winced at the bright light, shading his eyes with one hand. He anxiously tried to see the driver, but everything else besides the damned light was pitch black. The car inched forward and Dan backed up, panicking. His balance wavered, his fingers brushing along the brick wall. *Go away!*

The car suddenly lurched backward and then sharply turned, speeding off into the night. Dan wildly looked around, his eyes blinded still from the light, unable to see a thing. His fingers caught against the uneven brick. He looked down. A brown stain was splattered along the brick. His hand quickly receded back towards his chest, and Dan cradled it as he backed away, a look of disgust painted on his face as his lip quivered. His back smashed against the opposite wall. His knees gave out and his body sank down to the cold damp ground. He glanced down to the hand that still held his wallet. He flipped it open, and his driver's license flashed at him.

He read all the information on the card. Why he didn't know, but it seemed like it was the only thing to do right at that moment. His name in bold letters, Daniel Braddock, was followed by every single physical attribute of himself. His eye color, hair color, height, weight. He imagined this boy, the one smiling dimwitted in the card. He imagined the conversation from his dream. *See you around Doc.* It was the way he said it with such a carefree attitude that made the words sound so foreign to Dan now. They could never have been uttered from his mouth like that. It wasn't possible anymore. He glanced back down at the card, looking down at the six digits separated by the forward slash mark. His birthday, the date that told the world that he was only just in his twenties, seemed to be the most important information on this card. *Who the hell should be dealing with any of this shit when they're only twenty?* Dan took a deep breath, a sob escaping from his lips. It echoed off the walls faintly, floating away into the night. He glanced back up at the brown stain. Such a dull color now from its original vibrant red, scrubbed at for days but not completely clean. Dan wondered what the information of her driver's license would have read. Was she younger than him, older? What color eyes did she have, what color hair? But more importantly, what was her name. He wanted to put a name to that face that kept haunting him. A glow appeared from the left, and another car suddenly appeared. Dan leaped to his feet, crawling back into the dark corner of the alley.

A drop of water fell down his neck from the drainpipe above, a single line running down his back, chilling him to the bone. The car slowed down, ever so slowly easing forward when it came up to the alley. *They know, oh god they know! They know I'm here. They have Jamie and they know I'm here. Why did I come here? What the hell is wrong with me?* The car drove off, not even a hint of hostility in it. Dan took a deep breath, the last wave of dread washing through him in another layer of sweat.

It all suddenly came together in one fell swoop. The message, the tapes, the empty conversations that led in no direction all repeated themselves in his ears. Her face, Fuller's doubt, his parents forced hopes, all were images in his head. His own panic, the sinking feeling that every car that followed him was them, the feeling that no matter how much he tried to forget that night, it would still come back. It couldn't get rid of it. All these things suddenly rushed forth towards him like an enemy line charging forth. *Enough*, he thought. But it wasn't enough. His fingers brushed the brown brick, the stain that had fading from its ungodly red, but still bore the scar.

"Enough," he whispered. The word wasn't enough to stop it. His heart was bounding, his eyes squeezed shut till the colors all ran as one inside his head. Her body still lingered in front of him, her face inches from his. He heard a car in the distance start up, and felt it turn in his direction. He thrust his wallet back into his pocket, running his hand along the other personal items he kept with him.

"Enough."

But the second time was even weaker than the first, and the images still hurtled towards, the sounds of everyone important to him just ran as jumbled lyrics with no sense of order, getting louder and louder till they were drowning in the same sorrow that he felt. His fingernails were pinching his skin, his eyes peering from his fingers to look at the street. The headlights, once two separate lights were drawing closer into one as the car drew nearer. It was the endless pounding of his heart; it could be heard in his head, within his shaking fingers, his chest and all the way down to his feet. *Dan, I need your help!* It was all too much. He withdrew his hands, throwing them down at his sides as he raised his head, letting out a guttural howl.

"ENOUGH!"

# XX

Dan's roommate lit up the cigarette. The tiny flame licked the edges of the lighter for a brief second, slithering up onto his finger. The miniscule amount of heat that thrashed against his skin didn't faze him as he lit the cigarette, watching as his inhale made the flicker of flame ignite deeper into the rolled paper. He exhaled. Tendrils of smoke issued out softly from the end of the mini white stick. For a moment he imagined the smoke being sucked back in. The shards of glass molding and melting back together. But the smoke didn't recede back. In fact, it expanded more and more into the open air, fleeing the scene, but without great urgency.

His fingers already twitched as the taste of nicotine coursed through his lungs, his fidgeting body bounced a little more as the buzz washed through him like a calming shower after a massively horrific nightmare. *God damn it! Almost eight months without smoking and then I live with that crazy bastard! That son of a bitch!* A whole string of obscenities rushed through his mind, knowing that none of it was going to hit the rewind button and change it all. But it still felt good to finally freely think what thoughts had been creepy in his mind this whole time.

He took a huge inhale, feeling his lungs expand till they ballooned out as far as they could go. A pain settled in the pit of his stomach. The smoke trickled out his mouth, seeping through the cracks of his lips. He played with the cigarette, twirling it in his fingers as he watched the paper slowly burn away, crispy edges being taken by the slight breeze. It wasn't the product itself that was addictive to him. It was the feeling after. The alluring calmness that would blanket him, as if all the noise were ripped from the world, though the most chaotic scene would be occurring around him. He could be standing in a claustrophobic, windowless room with thirty screaming people, and he'd be serenely in the center without being distracted by a single sound.

The cigarette was finished, completely annihilated within minutes. He threw the butt onto the sidewalk, turned and faced the doorway to the apartment complex. A sudden dread seeped up in a heated wave. All the courage that he had stored away was gone. It was hardly courage at all it was fleeting so fast. *Just go in!* He told himself this over and over again, but his feet were still thick boulders. *It was nothing, he just freaked out for a second. Dan's not crazy, right?*

It took him a full ten minutes to force himself up those steps, to reach the door and swing it open. The room was quiet. Deathly still. It wasn't a trifling silence, but rather a soundlessness that he'd remember for years to come without ever being able to properly label it. Everything seemed perfectly in place, but cracked internally. The glass still lay there in pieces, as if fallen into place like it always should have been there in the center of the floor. It was as if Dan's coming apart at the seams was conventional, not out of the ordinary.

"Dan?" Why did he whisper the name? He didn't know why he inquired, why he made an attempt to communicate with another person. He was poised, ready for anything to bounce and attack him. No one else was in the apartment. The hesitant question was hurriedly answered with silence, and it was the only answer given. A glimpse at the ground and he picked up the discarded phone. It blinked wildly, begging to be addressed instead of so carelessly dismissed. Three missed calls were listed. He contemplated opening the phone to see whom, but then realized he had already dabbled way too deep into this mess. The apartment looked as if it had just been raided, and he had been wiped clean of everything he knew. He tripped on his way over to the window; his hand fell onto the cold windowpane. The glass surrounding his fingers began to cloud with condensation from the warmth of his fingertips. He could see birds fly outside but didn't hear them. A car drove past, exhaust spilling out in a moist cloud. But there was no sound. He was outside looking in. He was something inside nothing. He just wanted to get out. And never look back.

Dan held onto the cold metal bars. It was the only thing that felt real to him anymore, though his fingers seemed to hold nothing the bars were so intangible. His body felt weighed down by the lightweight sheet draped over him. His feet didn't reach the end of the rusty bed, so he instead had wrapped his fingers around the metal headboard. He felt tired but couldn't sleep. The second he closed his eyes suddenly a burst of energy ran through him. The contradicting feelings were excruciating.

The ceiling was gray except for the long brown line that stained half of the white paint. It was an ugly sore against a perfectly pale palate. His eyes, red and swollen, traced the stain over and over again. Nothing else came to mind except seeing her die over and over again. His fingers turned white as he wrung them tightly against the bars, the cold metal searing into his skin like hot iron. The uneven metal dug into his skin. It pressed into his skin, giving off the stomach wrenching feeling of a cigarette pushed into his arm. It seethed and burned and lingered. Frustration welled until an angry scream escaped his lips. He screamed till he couldn't breathe, breaking his cut fingers from the bars to hide his face. He felt the warm blood against his cold fingers dry instantly, his body so frozen and numb. It felt like hell, this place that held nothing.

It was an unsettling feeling that swept over them. The notion that their son opted from communicating at all was disheartening. Even further, it was the fact that he held them with nooses around their necks, able to have complete and utter power over them. If they were to call they would seem needy, so they just had to sit and wait patiently. The procedure was torturous. It started an endless train of emotions, ranging from anger to disappointment, discouragement to worry. At the expense of giving him space, they realized how much closer they really wanted him to be.

It wasn't that he didn't call every single day to say hello. It was that there was suddenly no more communication at all. His mother left numerous messages, to which Dan ignored them all. They both understood that it was nearing finals, drawing towards the break, back to the dangerous freedom of summer. Maybe once he was home everything would settle back again. The year had finally taken a toll on the family. Something still wasn't fixed with Dan, as much as they hated to admit it. The word "cure" held too much stigma to it, but it was the only word they could think about. The notion that he was sick, and needed to get healthy tore away at their insides, ripping them to pieces. But they couldn't deny it any longer.

So a strange determination suddenly existed between Dan's parents. They were hell bent on seeing their son act like himself again, never willing to give up until there was no more use. Wasn't that the nature of parents, to see that their children were happy and healthy? There was nothing wrong with not accepting that Dan had changed. He had made an effort for help; he just needed a little push. This determination stuck with them for a pathetic week, and then it faded into pure helplessness. It drove his mom nuts, to the point that she was deliberately hiding her phone so she wouldn't call him. His dad would stare at his doorway for brief seconds during the day, hearing the clock tick away with its hand pointing and laughing.

The strain that Dan's absence placed on his parents suddenly became more apparent. They wouldn't speak in the morning. His father would wake up, shower and immediately retreat to the kitchen, where he would force food down his throat for the mere sustenance he wished it could provide. He would hear his wife's alarm, and become scared that he would have to mumble even in a word to her. Likewise, Dan's mother wouldn't dare look her husband in the eye. They would both leave for work like this, and would return back to the house in just the same matter.

The evenings were even worse. As time progressed onward,

unable to stop for the family to be able to catch their breaths and relax, Emily began asking relentless questions about Dan's whereabouts. Father and mother came up with benign answers, feigned explanations that Dan was busy finishing up the semester of school. The skeptic look that developed in their daughter's eyes couldn't be ignored, and the cryptic look in theirs was just as fully established. They told her to drop it, but she kept coming at them, persistent and resolute. The incident in which her father finally screamed at her, yelling that he didn't want to talk about Dan for the rest of the night finally silenced Emily. It was set a completely new tone within the household.

Dan was taboo. The topic of Dan, the discussion of why he hadn't called, the prospect that maybe tonight would be the night that he finally would, all of it was not allowed to be spoken aloud. He was the sick relative that no one wanted to talk about. He was the teenager who had started dealing drugs to his friends and had gotten hopelessly hooked onto the substance as well. He was the obnoxious, over-dramatic aspiring artist with whom no one wanted to associate with cause deep down inside of that boy was a freak. His father finally accepted the fact that his son officially didn't want to return home that summer. His mother still shivered with discomfort every time she was answered by his voicemail, but she still felt the last grip of strength fighting for Dan, justifying his actions. Every so often Emily would trail into his room, empty and dark. She would stand in the lit up doorway, glance around and then softly close the door behind her.

It wasn't that they forgot about their son. That was never a possibility for any of them. But ignoring their situation was their way of coping. The truth seemed much harder to take than simply walking through life as nothing had changed. So for as long as they could, this was exactly what they did.

After his scream died, he sucked in a deep breath, but it didn't relax his body. *Anything, show me anything so I know where I am!*

217

His mind shouted this over and over. The sheet around him was strangling him, but he didn't have the will to even strip that off him and sit up. The bed, the sheet, even the streak of brown running down the ceiling like a trail of dried, cracked blood, were all like images from a dream, faintly lingering but fading so fast that he couldn't remember their exact existence or reality. *Were they always here? The bars didn't seem as cold anymore. Was I always holding onto them?* It was only the notion that what he actually saw had to be there that calmed him. And it was after that moment of analyzing everything in the room, that he suddenly realized where he was, and what he did to arrive here. The memory formed as vividly as the scars that were laden all over his body, scars from everything that had happened. His breathing stilled, a wave of peace suddenly settling over him.

Someone was here.

Dan closed his eyes, opened them and peered up. No one. He threw his head back down on his pillow. He felt no fear, no anger anymore. Nothing. Nothing but the feeling of peace, serenity.

Every so often, triggered by a random event, Fuller would look back at the copious amount of patients that he treated over the years. He would remember the patients that were extremely easy to get along with, the patients that he had first seen when he began his career, and still was seeing. He would remember the patients who told the most dramatic stories about what they were imagining or seeing, the patients who would have break downs in his office, and the patients that were so ridiculous they just made him laugh. There was always the group of the patients he didn't want to remember, or wished he didn't have to remember. They periodically made visits when he would find himself in these nostalgic sessions. They never left, and their words and conversations were the ones that he could remember verbatim, never leaving any detail out.

On the particular day that he fell into his period of reminiscence, it was generated by a phone call that woke him up thirty minutes earlier than what his alarm was set for. It wasn't that he was mad about having to come in earlier to deal with a situation. It was the annoying fact that it was merely thirty minutes before he would have been up anyways. If it was only thirty minutes, why didn't they just let him come in at the usual time? Or, if it were completely necessary, why not call him hours before, so that he was better able to understand the severity of the situation?

Walking in a fog, he entered his office. He went through the common routine of taking off his jacket, unpacking files from his bag, and setting up the coffee maker. It was all the actions of a normal day. The coffee maker sputtered to life, admitting forth tendrils of steam into the room. The fragment smell of coffee was strong, the aroma filling the entire room. Fuller sat down at his desk, waking up his computer and settling down for another day.

But this day was different. The phone blinked wildly, as if spastic. The computer screen lit up with a dozen emails, some forwarded and some sent directly to him, but many of them held the red exclamation point of high importance. An unease gripped Fuller as he suddenly realized the real reason that he was called in early. Files were suddenly appearing in his office, and phone calls were made so that he could properly explain what was happening. Throughout all of this he was given no real amount of time to digest any of it. Hours of this dismantled array of work and shambled organization continued. Fuller never had a chance to grab the cup of coffee that was still being heated by the coffee maker at the other end of his office. He never ate, never took a minute to sigh, turn around and look out at the grounds of the hospital from his window. The sun rose, was covered by thick clouds, and then began to set, all without Fuller even giving it a second's glance. The sun felt abandoned that day, and the sky clouded over and threatened rain.

A package had been delivered during the time span of the foreboding day. It was marked with official seals and stamps, but contained only one single item. Wrapped in cheap plastic lining, Fuller unwound the cassette tape from its trappings, setting it down on the desk in front of him. It was the way the tape arrived that disturbed him. It was hand delivered. It was planned. Fuller stared at the tape for a few minutes, his neck and back craned as far back into his seat as they could go, as if the tape would suddenly start to shake and come to life right before his eyes. He finally proceeded to pick up the tape, inspecting every inch of it. The hard plastic casing, the strip of worn brown film, none of it revealed any more information. It was like a compliant tortured soul, clamped up and silent, refusing to relinquish any more secrets. The torturer would have to break him down till only little breaths lingered in his lungs, and those little breaths would finally utter the words that needed to be heard.

A speck of dirt lingered near the printed label that was stickered to one side of the tape, which only bore Fuller's name. It was addressed to him, like a personal vendetta against every effort that he had made these past few months. It laughed and mocked him. Fuller without difficulty brushed off the piece of dirt from the tape. And it was in that simplicity that he knew it was all over. The tape was suddenly just a tape, plain looking and without any riddles. This was all that was left to listen to.

The tape sat in front of Fuller for a very long time before he finally stood up with a gradual sense of presentiment clinging to his feet. Everything about anything was in this tape, and it all dealt with one single patient. Just one person and the entire outcome lived in the few recorded minutes of the tape. These were the moments when Fuller hated his job, when he absolutely despised it and wanted nothing more to do then stand up and shout at the top of his lungs that this was a fucked up world and there was nothing more that he could do. He walked to the stereo system, pressing the button that released the tape deck as if it were a gateway to a fortress being slowly lowered open by metal chains, finally allowing the annoyed tape to finally express itself. The cassette clicked as it slide into the player, and with a sharp snap Fuller closed the player.

The phone rang, a loud blaring noise, making Fuller jump slightly though he didn't turn to face the ugly machine. Fuller knew exactly who it was going to be. The screams, the shouts, the blame. It was too much for him. He absentmindedly walked to his desk without really looking at it, picked up the phone and set it back down on the receiver. He turned his attention back to the tape, turning the system on, taking a deep breath. He looked at the blurred single window of the tape player, where his name on the label of the cassette tape stared back him with the same distorted vision. No matter how many minutes he stood here in front of the system he knew that he would never be fully ready or prepared to hear what had to be said. So he pushed the play button, and listened as a voice droned out of the speakers. It started off softly, but gained strength and resistance towards the end. The voice gained purpose and reason, though it still shook every so often with an unquenchable fear.

It was played out perfectly. The actions, the signs, the words. It was like an immense amount of foreshadowing had been thrust upon him and he ignored it all. It had the perfect player, the perfect actor. It had the suspense, the downfall and the conclusion. The only thing it lacked was a perfect ending. An ending in which, though left shocked, the audience still felt something. An ending that played perfect music for the people to process out with, an ending that left one with thoughts and interpretations. One that left the audience satisfied. Nothing about this was satisfying.

*"No one can imagine what it's like to see someone killed. We picture it all the time. We see characters killed all the time in movies. We watch people get stabbed, shot, tortured, mutilated till even their last breath is agonizing. But there's always a point, when you feel yourself get sucked into too much, that you can close your eyes and remember that it's only a movie. When you finally see someone get killed, you can't close your eyes and wish it all away. A body seems impenetrable. A cut heals within days. A broken bone can be strapped back into place. But a bullet to the head can't heal."*

*"Once shot, the mind shuts off. The blood pools to a heavy thickness around the wound and spills from the body we once thought was indestructible. The bullet can be removed, but if close enough, the damage is already done and person is already dead. A second passes and that is all the victim has. The person can take a breath, a last look and then that's it. Then there's nothing."*

*"When a person gets stabbed, the insides don't magically blend back to their original position. If the murderer cuts enough tissue, muscle, arteries, the victim bleeds to death. If a throat is slashed, one sees more blood pool from a single slash mark than they thought possible. A stab in the arm or leg could be fixed. But what about the tendons that are ripped? What about the lips that are torn apart as the knife strikes up along the cheek?"*

*"When a person thinks about death, we don't think about the cold hard metal that easily breaks flesh. Hopefully a person can think about peacefully closing aged eyes and never waking up. But when a person is murdered, they don't get that happy feeling. Instead, they are covered in agony, pain and twisted fate. Suddenly it isn't a scene in a movie that can be skipped, it isn't the horror story that gives us a nightmare for only one night, or the video game that can be shut off. It's only a moment that the victim has, and then it's over. So tell me, what do you envision now when someone dies?"*

*"This kill is all I see now."*

The voice died out, a shuffle of movement. Then the tape sharply stopped and began to rewind.

That was all that was recorded.

———————————————————————————————

"Dan?" her voice appeared. No other sound was there but her voice. And it didn't shock Dan. He looked up and saw Jamie's pretty face. They stared in silence for quite some time. She gingerly sat at the edge of the bed, holding her steady gaze. There was no quiver in her, just a resolution, the same that had suddenly formed into his eyes. "How long have you been here?" she asked earnestly, though she had been waiting for him all this time. "How long, Dan?"

The minutes for everyone else were practically spanning over another lifespan for him.

"Not long."

She smiled. A welcoming, beckoning smile.

"I missed you Dan." Dan sat up, reaching over to graze her hand, to make sure she was there. She was, but yet so was he.

"No one can imagine what it's like to see someone killed…"

**FIN**

Rachel Ann Chrostowski

# ABOUT THE AUTHOR

Rachel Ann Chrostowski grew up in Waukesha, Wisconsin. She attended Marquette University in the Fall of 2008. There she met Garrett I. Lenz and the two became great friends. In the Spring of 2010, Garrett came up with the idea for the story, and was quick to include Rachel. She wrote diligently while still seeking two degrees at Marquette. After months of writing and re-writing, the story began taking shape and eventually developed into something with more layers and hidden messages than any reader will be able to decrypt. At the age of twenty-four, this is Rachel's first published novel.

www.ingramcontent.com/pod-product-compliance
Lightning Source LLC
Chambersburg PA
CBHW060317260626
47160CB00007B/2643